I0554250

Tommy and Co

JEROME K. JEROME

Author of "Paul Kelver," "Idle Thoughts of an Idle Fellow,"
"Three Men in a Boat," etc.

Serenity
Publishers, LLC

ROCKVILLE, MARYLAND

2011

ISBN: 978-1-60450-834-5

Published by Serenity Publishers
An Arc Manor Company
P. O. Box 10339
Rockville, MD 20849-0339
www.SerenityPublishers.com
Printed in the United States of America/United Kingdom

CONTENTS

STORY THE FIRST

Peter Hope Plans His Prospectus

"COME IN!" said Peter Hope.

Peter Hope was tall and thin, clean-shaven but for a pair of side whiskers close-cropped and terminating just below the ear, with hair of the kind referred to by sympathetic barbers as "getting a little thin on the top, sir," but arranged w ith economy, that everywhere is poverty's true helpmate. About Mr. Peter Hope's linen, which was white though somewhat frayed, there was a self-assertiveness that invariably arrested the attention of even the most casual observer. Decidedly there was too much of it—its ostentation aided and abetted by the retiring nature of the cut away coat, whose chief aim clearly was to slip off and disappear behind its owner's back. "I'm a poor old thing," it seemed to say. "I don't shine—or, rather, I shine too much among these up-to-date young modes. I only hamper you. You would be much more comfortable without me." To persuade it to accompany him, its proprietor had to employ force, keeping fastened the lowest of its three buttons. At every step, it struggled for its liberty. Another characteristic of Peter's, linking him to the past, was his black silk cravat, secured by a couple of gold pins chained together. Watching him as he now sat writing, his long legs encased in tightly strapped grey trousering, crossed beneath the table, the lamplight falling on his fresh-complexioned face, upon the shapely hand that steadied the half-written sheet, a stranger might have rubbed his eyes, wondering by what hallucination he thus found himself in presence seemingly of some young beau belonging to the early 'forties; but looking closer, would have seen the many wrinkles.

"Come in!" repeated Mr. Peter Hope, raising his voice, but not his eyes.

The door opened, and a small, white face, out of which gleamed a pair of bright, black eyes, was thrust sideways into the room.

"Come in!" repeated Mr. Peter Hope for the third time. "Who is it?"

A hand not over clean, grasping a greasy cloth cap, appeared below the face.

"Not ready yet," said Mr. Hope. "Sit down and wait."

The door opened wider, and the whole of the figure slid in and, closing the door behind it, sat itself down upon the extreme edge of the chair nearest.

"Which are you—*Central News* or *Courier*?" demanded Mr. Peter Hope, but without looking up from his work.

The bright, black eyes, which had just commenced an examination of the room by a careful scrutiny of the smoke-grimed ceiling, descended and fixed themselves upon the one clearly defined bald patch upon his head that, had he been aware of it, would have troubled Mr. Peter Hope. But the full, red lips beneath the turned-up nose remained motionless.

That he had received no answer to his question appeared to have escaped the attention of Mr. Peter Hope. The thin, white hand moved steadily to and fro across the paper. Three more sheets were added to those upon the floor. Then Mr. Peter Hope pushed back his chair and turned his gaze for the first time upon his visitor.

To Peter Hope, hack journalist, long familiar with the genus Printer's Devil, small white faces, tangled hair, dirty hands, and greasy caps were common objects in the neighbourhood of that buried rivulet, the Fleet. But this was a new species. Peter Hope sought his spectacles, found them after some trouble under a heap of newspapers, adjusted them upon his high, arched nose, leant forward, and looked long and up and down.

"God bless my soul!" said Mr. Peter Hope. "What is it?"

The figure rose to its full height of five foot one and came forward slowly.

Over a tight-fitting garibaldi of blue silk, excessively *decollete*, it wore what once had been a boy's pepper-and-salt jacket. A worsted comforter wound round the neck still left a wide expanse of throat showing above the garibaldi. Below the jacket fell a long, black skirt, the train of which had been looped up about the waist and fastened with a cricket-belt.

"Who are you? What do you want?" asked Mr. Peter Hope.

For answer, the figure, passing the greasy cap into its other hand, stooped down and, seizing the front of the long skirt, began to haul it up.

"Don't do that!" said Mr. Peter Hope. "I say, you know, you—"

But by this time the skirt had practically disappeared, leaving to view a pair of much-patched trousers, diving into the right-hand pocket of which the dirty hand drew forth a folded paper, which, having opened and smoothed out, it laid upon the desk.

Mr. Peter Hope pushed up his spectacles till they rested on his eyebrows, and read aloud—"'Steak and Kidney Pie, *4d.*; Do. (large size), *6d.*; Boiled Mutton—'"

"That's where I've been for the last two weeks," said the figure,—"Hammond's Eating House!"

The listener noted with surprise that the voice—though it told him as plainly as if he had risen and drawn aside the red rep curtains, that outside in Gough Square the yellow fog lay like the ghost of a dead sea—betrayed no Cockney accent, found no difficulty with its aitches.

"You ask for Emma. She'll say a good word for me. She told me so."

"But, my good—" Mr. Peter Hope, checking himself, sought again the assistance of his glasses. The glasses being unable to decide the point, their owner had to put the question bluntly:

"Are you a boy or a girl?"

"I dunno."

"You don't know!"

"What's the difference?"

Mr. Peter Hope stood up, and taking the strange figure by the shoulders, turned it round slowly twice, apparently under the impression that the process might afford to him some clue. But it did not.

"What is your name?"

"Tommy."

"Tommy what?"

"Anything you like. I dunno. I've had so many of 'em."

7

"What do you want? What have you come for?"

"You're Mr. Hope, ain't you, second floor, 16, Gough Square?"

"That is my name."

"You want somebody to do for you?"

"You mean a housekeeper!"

"Didn't say anything about housekeeper. Said you wanted some-body to do for you—cook and clean the place up. Heard 'em talking about it in the shop this afternoon. Old lady in green bonnet was asking Mother Hammond if she knew of anyone."

"Mrs. Postwhistle—yes, I did ask her to look out for someone for me. Why, do you know of anyone? Have you been sent by anybody?"

"You don't want anything too 'laborate in the way o' cooking? You was a simple old chap, so they said; not much trouble."

"No—no. I don't want much—someone clean and respectable. But why couldn't she come herself? Who is it?"

"Well, what's wrong about me?"

"I beg your pardon," said Mr. Peter Hope.

"Why won't I do? I can make beds and clean rooms—all that sort o' thing. As for cooking, I've got a natural aptitude for it. You ask Emma; she'll tell you. You don't want nothing 'laborate?"

"Elizabeth," said Mr. Peter Hope, as he crossed and, taking up the poker, proceeded to stir the fire, "are we awake or asleep?"

Elizabeth thus appealed to, raised herself on her hind legs and dug her claws into her master's thigh. Mr. Hope's trousers being thin, it was the most practical answer she could have given him.

"Done a lot of looking after other people for their benefit," con-tinued Tommy. "Don't see why I shouldn't do it for my own."

"My dear—I do wish I knew whether you were a boy or a girl. Do you seriously suggest that I should engage you as my housekeep-er?" asked Mr. Peter Hope, now upright with his back to the fire.

"I'd do for you all right," persisted Tommy. "You give me my grub and a shake-down and, say, sixpence a week, and I'll grumble less than most of 'em."

"Don't be ridiculous," said Mr. Peter Hope.

"You won't try me?"

"Of course not; you must be mad."

"All right. No harm done." The dirty hand reached out towards the desk, and possessing itself again of Hammond's Bill of Fare, commenced the operations necessary for bearing it away in safety.

"Here's a shilling for you," said Mr. Peter Hope.

"Rather not," said Tommy. "Thanks all the same."

"Nonsense!" said Mr. Peter Hope.

"Rather not," repeated Tommy. "Never know where that sort of thing may lead you to."

"All right," said Mr. Peter Hope, replacing the coin in his pocket. "Don't!"

The figure moved towards the door.

"Wait a minute. Wait a minute," said Mr. Peter Hope irritably.

The figure, with its hand upon the door, stood still.

"Are you going back to Hammond's?"

"No. I've finished there. Only took me on for a couple o' weeks, while one of the gals was ill. She came back this morning."

"Who are your people?"

Tommy seemed puzzled. "What d'ye mean?"

"Well, whom do you live with?"

"Nobody."

"You've got nobody to look after you—to take care of you?"

"Take care of me! D'ye think I'm a bloomin' kid?"

"Then where are you going to now?"

"Going? Out."

Peter Hope's irritation was growing.

"I mean, where are you going to sleep? Got any money for a lodging?"

"Yes, I've got some money," answered Tommy. "But I don't think much o' lodgings. Not a particular nice class as you meet there. I shall sleep out to-night. 'Tain't raining."

Elizabeth uttered a piercing cry.

"Serves you right!" growled Peter savagely. "How can anyone help treading on you when you will get just between one's legs. Told you of it a hundred times."

The truth of the matter was that Peter was becoming very angry with himself. For no reason whatever, as he told himself, his memory would persist in wandering to Ilford Cemetery, in a certain desolate corner of which lay a fragile little woman whose lungs had been but ill adapted to breathing London fogs; with, on the top of her, a still smaller and still more fragile mite of humanity that, in compliment to its only relative worth a penny-piece, had been christened Thomas—a name common enough in all conscience, as

Peter had reminded himself more than once. In the name of common sense, what had dead and buried Tommy Hope to do with this affair? The whole thing was the veriest sentiment, and sentiment was Mr. Peter Hope's abomination. Had he not penned articles innumerable pointing out its baneful influence upon the age? Had he not always condemned it, wherever he had come across it in play or book? Now and then the suspicion had crossed Peter's mind that, in spite of all this, he was somewhat of a sentimentalist himself—things had suggested this to him. The fear had always made him savage.

"You wait here till I come back," he growled, seizing the astonished Tommy by the worsted comforter and spinning it into the centre of the room. "Sit down, and don't you dare to move." And Peter went out and slammed the door behind him.

"Bit off his chump, ain't he?" remarked Tommy to Elizabeth, as the sound of Peter's descending footsteps died away. People had a way of addressing remarks to Elizabeth. Something in her manner invited this.

"Oh, well, it's all in the day's work," commented Tommy cheerfully, and sat down as bid.

Five minutes passed, maybe ten. Then Peter returned, accompanied by a large, restful lady, to whom surprise—one felt it instinctively—had always been, and always would remain, an unknown quantity.

Tommy rose.

"That's the—the article," explained Peter.

Mrs. Postwhistle compressed her lips and slightly tossed her head. It was the attitude of not ill-natured contempt from which she regarded most human affairs.

"That's right," said Mrs. Postwhistle; "I remember seeing 'er there—leastways, it was an 'er right enough then. What 'ave you done with your clothes?"

"They weren't mine," explained Tommy. "They were things what Mrs. Hammond had lent me."

"Is that your own?" asked Mrs. Postwhistle, indicating the blue silk garibaldi.

"Yes."

"What went with it?"

"Tights. They were too far gone."

"What made you give up the tumbling business and go to Mrs. 'Ammond's?"

"It gave me up. Hurt myself."

"Who were you with last?"

"Martini troupe."

"And before that?"

"Oh! heaps of 'em."

"Nobody ever told you whether you was a boy or a girl?"

"Nobody as I'd care to believe. Some of them called me the one, some of them the other. It depended upon what was wanted."

"How old are you?"

"I dunno."

Mrs. Postwhistle turned to Peter, who was jingling keys.

"Well, there's the bed upstairs. It's for you to decide."

"What I don't want to do," explained Peter, sinking his voice to a confidential whisper, "is to make a fool of myself."

"That's always a good rule," agreed Mrs. Postwhistle, "for those to whom it's possible."

"Anyhow," said Peter, "one night can't do any harm. To-morrow we can think what's to be done."

"To-morrow" had always been Peter's lucky day. At the mere mention of the magic date his spirits invariably rose. He now turned upon Tommy a countenance from which all hesitation was banished.

"Very well, Tommy," said Mr. Peter Hope, "you can sleep here to-night. Go with Mrs. Postwhistle, and she'll show you your room."

The black eyes shone.

"You're going to give me a trial?"

"We'll talk about all that to-morrow." The black eyes clouded.

"Look here. I tell you straight, it ain't no good."

"What do you mean? What isn't any good?" demanded Peter.

"You'll want to send me to prison."

"To prison!"

"Oh, yes. You'll call it a school, I know. You ain't the first that's tried that on. It won't work." The bright, black eyes were flashing passionately. "I ain't done any harm. I'm willing to work. I can keep myself. I always have. What's it got to do with anybody else?"

Had the bright, black eyes retained their expression of passionate defiance, Peter Hope might have retained his common sense. Only Fate arranged that instead they should suddenly fill with wild tears. And at sight of them Peter's common sense went out of the room disgusted, and there was born the history of many things.

"Don't be silly," said Peter. "You didn't understand. Of course I'm going to give you a trial. You're going to 'do' for me. I merely meant that we'd leave the details till to-morrow. Come, housekeepers don't cry."

The little wet face looked up.

"You mean it? Honour bright?"

"Honour bright. Now go and wash yourself. Then you shall get me my supper."

The odd figure, still heaving from its paroxysm of sobs, stood up.

"And I have my grub, my lodging, and sixpence a week?"

"Yes, yes; I think that's a fair arrangement," agreed Mr. Peter Hope, considering. "Don't you, Mrs. Postwhistle?"

"With a frock—or a suit of trousers—thrown in," suggested Mrs. Postwhistle. "It's generally done."

"If it's the custom, certainly," agreed Mr. Peter Hope. "Sixpence a week and clothes."

And this time it was Peter that, in company with Elizabeth, sat waiting the return of Tommy.

"I rather hope," said Peter, "it's a boy. It was the fogs, you know. If only I could have afforded to send him away!"

Elizabeth looked thoughtful. The door opened.

"Ah! that's better, much better," said Mr. Peter Hope. "'Pon my word, you look quite respectable."

By the practical Mrs. Postwhistle a working agreement, benefiting both parties, had been arrived at with the long-trained skirt; while an ample shawl arranged with judgment disguised the nakedness that lay below. Peter, a fastidious gentleman, observed with satisfaction that the hands, now clean, had been well cared for.

"Give me that cap," said Peter. He threw it in the glowing fire. It burned brightly, diffusing strange odours.

"There's a travelling cap of mine hanging up in the passage. You can wear that for the present. Take this half-sovereign and get me some cold meat and beer for supper. You'll find everything else you want in that sideboard or else in the kitchen. Don't ask me a hundred questions, and don't make a noise," and Peter went back to his work.

"Good idea, that half-sovereign," said Peter. "Shan't be bothered with 'Master Tommy' any more, don't expect. Starting a nursery at our time of life. Madness." Peter's pen scratched and spluttered. Elizabeth kept an eye upon the door.

"Quarter of an hour," said Peter, looking at his watch. "Told you so." The article on which Peter was now engaged appeared to be of a worrying nature.

"Then why," said Peter, "why did he refuse that shilling? Artfulness," concluded Peter, "pure artfulness. Elizabeth, old girl, we've got out of this business cheaply. Good idea, that half-sovereign." Peter gave vent to a chuckle that had the effect of alarming Elizabeth.

But luck evidently was not with Peter that night.

"Pingle's was sold out," explained Tommy, entering with parcels; "had to go to Bow's in Farringdon Street."

"Oh!" said Peter, without looking up.

Tommy passed through into the little kitchen behind. Peter wrote on rapidly, making up for lost time.

"Good!" murmured Peter, smiling to himself, "that's a neat phrase. That ought to irritate them."

Now, as he wrote, while with noiseless footsteps Tommy, unseen behind him, moved to and fro and in and out the little kitchen, there came to Peter Hope this very curious experience: it felt to him as if for a long time he had been ill—so ill as not even to have been aware of it—and that now he was beginning to be himself again; consciousness of things returning to him. This solidly furnished, long, oak-panelled room with its air of old-world dignity and repose—this sober, kindly room in which for more than half his life he had lived and worked—why had he forgotten it? It came forward greeting him with an amused smile, as of some old friend long parted from. The faded photos, in stiff, wooden frames upon the chimney-piece, among them that of the fragile little woman with the unadaptable lungs.

"God bless my soul!" said Mr. Peter Hope, pushing back his chair. "It's thirty years ago. How time does fly! Why, let me see, I must be—"

"D'you like it with a head on it?" demanded Tommy, who had been waiting patiently for signs.

Peter shook himself awake and went to his supper.

A bright idea occurred to Peter in the night. "Of course; why didn't I think of it before? Settle the question at once." Peter fell into an easy sleep.

"Tommy," said Peter, as he sat himself down to breakfast the next morning. "By-the-by," asked Peter with a puzzled expression, putting down his cup, "what is this?"

"Cauffee," informed him Tommy. "You said cauffee."

"Oh!" replied Peter. "For the future, Tommy, if you don't mind, I will take tea of a morning."

"All the same to me," explained the agreeable Tommy, "it's your breakfast."

"What I was about to say," continued Peter, "was that you're not looking very well, Tommy."

"I'm all right," asserted Tommy; "never nothing the matter with me."

"Not that you know of, perhaps; but one can be in a very bad way, Tommy, without being aware of it. I cannot have anyone about me that I am not sure is in thoroughly sound health."

"If you mean you've changed your mind and want to get rid of me—" began Tommy, with its chin in the air.

"I don't want any of your uppishness," snapped Peter, who had wound himself up for the occasion to a degree of assertiveness that surprised even himself. "If you are a thoroughly strong and healthy person, as I think you are, I shall be very glad to retain your services. But upon that point I must be satisfied. It is the custom," explained Peter. "It is always done in good families. Run round to this address"—Peter wrote it upon a leaf of his notebook—"and ask Dr. Smith to come and see me before he begins his round. You go at once, and don't let us have any argument."

"That is the way to talk to that young person—clearly," said Peter to himself, listening to Tommy's footsteps dying down the stairs.

Hearing the street-door slam, Peter stole into the kitchen and brewed himself a cup of coffee.

Dr. Smith, who had commenced life as Herr Schmidt, but who in consequence of difference of opinion with his Government was now an Englishman with strong Tory prejudices, had but one sorrow: it was that strangers would mistake him for a foreigner. He was short and stout, with bushy eyebrows and a grey moustache, and looked so fierce that children cried when they saw him, until he patted them on the head and addressed them as "mein leedle frent" in a voice so soft and tender that they had to leave off howling just to wonder where it came from. He and Peter, who was a vehement Radical, had been cronies for many years, and had each an indulgent contempt for the other's understanding, tempered by a sincere affection for one another they would have found it difficult to account for.

"What tink you is de matter wid de leedle wench?" demanded Dr. Smith, Peter having opened the case. Peter glanced round the room. The kitchen door was closed.

"How do you know it's a wench?"

The eyes beneath the bushy brows grew rounder. "If id is not a wench, why dress it—"

"Haven't dressed it," interrupted Peter. "Just what I'm waiting to do—so soon as I know."

And Peter recounted the events of the preceding evening.

Tears gathered in the doctor's small, round eyes. His absurd sentimentalism was the quality in his friend that most irritated Peter.

"Poor leedle waif!" murmured the soft-hearted old gentleman. "Id was de good Providence dat guided her—or him, whichever id be."

"Providence be hanged!" snarled Peter. "What was my Providence doing—landing me with a gutter-brat to look after?"

"So like you Radicals," sneered the doctor, "to despise a fellow human creature just because id may not have been born in burble and fine linen."

"I didn't send for you to argue politics," retorted Peter, controlling his indignation by an effort. "I want you to tell me whether it's a boy or a girl, so that I may know what to do with it."

"What mean you to do wid id?" inquired the doctor.

"I don't know," confessed Peter. "If it's a boy, as I rather think it is, maybe I'll be able to find it a place in one of the offices—after I've taught it a little civilisation."

"And if id be a girl?"

"How can it be a girl when it wears trousers?" demanded Peter. "Why anticipate difficulties?"

Peter, alone, paced to and fro the room, his hands behind his back, his ear on the alert to catch the slightest sound from above.

"I do hope it is a boy," said Peter, glancing up.

Peter's eyes rested on the photo of the fragile little woman gazing down at him from its stiff frame upon the chimney-piece. Thirty years ago, in this same room, Peter had paced to and fro, his hands behind his back, his ear alert to catch the slightest sound from above, had said to himself the same words.

"It's odd," mused Peter—"very odd indeed."

The door opened. The stout doctor, preceded at a little distance by his watch-chain, entered and closed the door behind him.

"A very healthy child," said the doctor, "as fine a child as any one could wish to see. A girl."

The two old gentlemen looked at one another. Elizabeth, possibly relieved in her mind, began to purr.

"What am I to do with it?" demanded Peter.

"A very awkward bosition for you," agreed the sympathetic doctor.

"I was a fool!" declared Peter.

"You haf no one here to look after de leedle wench when you are away," pointed out the thoughtful doctor.

"And from what I've seen of the imp," added Peter, "it will want some looking after."

"I tink—I tink," said the helpful doctor, "I see a way out!"

"What?"

The doctor thrust his fierce face forward and tapped knowingly with his right forefinger the right side of his round nose. "I will take charge of de leedle wench."

"You?"

"To me de case will not present de same difficulties. I haf a housekeeper."

"Oh, yes, Mrs. Whateley."

"She is a goot woman when you know her," explained the doctor. "She only wants managing."

"Pooh!" ejaculated Peter.

"Why do you say dat?" inquired the doctor.

"You! bringing up a headstrong girl. The idea!"

"I should be kind, but firm."

"You don't know her."

"How long haf you known her?"

"Anyhow, I'm not a soft-hearted sentimentalist that would just ruin the child."

"Girls are not boys," persisted the doctor; "dey want different treatment."

"Well, I'm not a brute!" snarled Peter. "Besides, suppose she turns out rubbish! What do you know about her?"

"I take my chance," agreed the generous doctor.

"It wouldn't be fair," retorted honest Peter.

"Tink it over," said the doctor. "A place is never home widout de leedle feet. We Englishmen love de home. You are different. You haf no sentiment."

"I cannot help feeling," explained Peter, "a sense of duty in this matter. The child came to me. It is as if this thing had been laid upon me."

"If you look upon id dat way, Peter," sighed the doctor.

"With sentiment," went on Peter, "I have nothing to do; but duty—duty is quite another thing." Peter, feeling himself an ancient Roman, thanked the doctor and shook hands with him.

Tommy, summoned, appeared.

"The doctor, Tommy," said Peter, without looking up from his writing, "gives a very satisfactory account of you. So you can stop."

"Told you so," returned Tommy. "Might have saved your money."

"But we shall have to find you another name."

"What for?"

"If you are to be a housekeeper, you must be a girl."

"Don't like girls."

"Can't say I think much of them myself, Tommy. We must make the best of it. To begin with, we must get you proper clothes."

"Hate skirts. They hamper you."

"Tommy," said Peter severely, "don't argue."

"Pointing out facts ain't arguing," argued Tommy. "They do hamper you. You try 'em."

The clothes were quickly made, and after a while they came to fit; but the name proved more difficult of adjustment. A sweet-faced, laughing lady, known to fame by a title respectable and orthodox, appears an honoured guest to-day at many a literary gathering. But the old fellows, pressing round, still call her "Tommy."

The week's trial came to an end. Peter, whose digestion was delicate, had had a happy thought.

"What I propose, Tommy—I mean Jane," said Peter, "is that we should get in a woman to do just the mere cooking. That will give you more time to—to attend to other things, Tommy—Jane, I mean."

"What other things?" chin in the air.

"The—the keeping of the rooms in order, Tommy. The—the dusting."

"Don't want twenty-four hours a day to dust four rooms."

"Then there are messages, Tommy. It would be a great advantage to me to have someone I could send on a message without feeling I was interfering with the housework."

"What are you driving at?" demanded Tommy. "Why, I don't have half enough to do as it is. I can do all—"

Peter put his foot down. "When I say a thing, I mean a thing. The sooner you understand that, the better. How dare you argue with me! Fiddle-de-dee!" For two pins Peter would have employed an expletive even stronger, so determined was he feeling.

Tommy without another word left the room. Peter looked at Elizabeth and winked.

Poor Peter! His triumph was short-lived. Five minutes later, Tommy returned, clad in the long, black skirt, supported by the cricket belt, the blue garibaldi cut *decollete*, the pepper-and-salt jacket, the worsted comforter, the red lips very tightly pressed, the long lashes over the black eyes moving very rapidly.

"Tommy" (severely), "what is this tomfoolery?"

"I understand. I ain't no good to you. Thanks for giving me a trial. My fault."

"Tommy" (less severely), "don't be an idiot."

"Ain't an idiot. 'Twas Emma. Told me I was good at cooking. Said I'd got an aptitude for it. She meant well."

"Tommy" (no trace of severity), "sit down. Emma was quite right. Your cooking is—is promising. As Emma puts it, you have aptitude. Your—perseverance, your hopefulness proves it."

"Then why d'ye want to get someone else in to do it?"

If Peter could have answered truthfully! If Peter could have replied:

"My dear, I am a lonely old gentleman. I did not know it until—until the other day. Now I cannot forget it again. Wife and child died many years ago. I was poor, or I might have saved them. That made me hard. The clock of my life stood still. I hid away the key. I did not want to think. You crept to me out of the cruel fog, awakened old dreams. Do not go away any more"—perhaps Tommy, in spite of her fierce independence, would have consented to be useful; and thus Peter might have gained his end at less cost of indigestion. But the penalty for being an anti-sentimentalist is that you must not talk like this even to yourself. So Peter had to cast about for other methods.

"Why shouldn't I keep two servants if I like?" It did seem hard on the old gentleman.

"What's the sense of paying two to do the work of one? You would only be keeping me on out of charity." The black eyes flashed. "I ain't a beggar."

"And you really think, Tommy—I should say Jane, you can manage the—the whole of it? You won't mind being sent on a message, perhaps in the very middle of your cooking. It was that I was thinking of, Tommy—some cooks would."

"You go easy," advised him Tommy, "till I complain of having too much to do."

Peter returned to his desk. Elizabeth looked up. It seemed to Peter that Elizabeth winked.

The fortnight that followed was a period of trouble to Peter, for Tommy, her suspicions having been aroused, was sceptical of "business" demanding that Peter should dine with this man at the club, lunch with this editor at the Cheshire Cheese. At once the chin would go up into the air, the black eyes cloud threateningly. Peter, an unmarried man for thirty years, lacking experience, would under cross-examination contradict himself, become confused, break down over essential points.

"Really," grumbled Peter to himself one evening, sawing at a mutton chop, "really there's no other word for it—I'm henpecked."

Peter that day had looked forward to a little dinner at a favourite restaurant, with his "dear old friend Blenkinsopp, a bit of a gourmet, Tommy—that means a man who likes what you would call elaborate cooking!"—forgetful at the moment that he had used up "Blenkinsopp" three days before for a farewell supper, "Blenkinsopp" having to set out the next morning for Egypt. Peter was not facile at invention. Names in particular had always been a difficulty to him.

"I like a spirit of independence," continued Peter to himself. "Wish she hadn't quite so much of it. Wonder where she got it from."

The situation was becoming more serious to Peter than he cared to admit. For day by day, in spite of her tyrannies, Tommy was growing more and more indispensable to Peter. Tommy was the first audience that for thirty years had laughed at Peter's jokes; Tommy was the first public that for thirty years had been convinced that Peter was the most brilliant journalist in Fleet Street; Tommy was the first anxiety that for thirty years had rendered it needful that Peter each night should mount stealthily the creaking stairs, steal with shaded candle to a bedside. If only Tommy wouldn't "do" for him! If only she could be persuaded to "do" something else.

Another happy thought occurred to Peter.

"Tommy—I mean Jane," said Peter, "I know what I'll do with you."

"What's the game now?"

"I'll make a journalist of you."

"Don't talk rot."

"It isn't rot. Besides, I won't have you answer me like that. As a Devil—that means, Tommy, the unseen person in the background that helps a journalist to do his work—you would be invaluable to me. It would pay me, Tommy—pay me very handsomely. I should make money out of you."

This appeared to be an argument that Tommy understood. Peter, with secret delight, noticed that the chin retained its normal level.

"I did help a chap to sell papers, once," remembered Tommy; "he said I was fly at it."

"I told you so," exclaimed Peter triumphantly. "The methods are different, but the instinct required is the same. We will get a woman in to relieve you of the housework."

The chin shot up into the air.

"I could do it in my spare time."

"You see, Tommy, I should want you to go about with me—to be always with me."

"Better try me first. Maybe you're making an error."

Peter was learning the wisdom of the serpent.

"Quite right, Tommy. We will first see what you can do. Perhaps, after all, it may turn out that you are better as a cook." In his heart Peter doubted this.

But the seed had fallen upon good ground. It was Tommy herself that manoeuvred her first essay in journalism. A great man had come to London—was staying in apartments especially prepared for him in St. James's Palace. Said every journalist in London to himself: "If I could obtain an interview with this Big Man, what a big thing it would be for me!" For a week past, Peter had carried everywhere about with him a paper headed: "Interview of Our Special Correspondent with Prince Blank," questions down left-hand column, very narrow; space for answers right-hand side, very wide. But the Big Man was experienced.

"I wonder," said Peter, spreading the neatly folded paper on the desk before him, "I wonder if there can be any way of getting at him—any dodge or trick, any piece of low cunning, any plausible lie that I haven't thought of."

"Old Man Martin—called himself Martini—was just such another," commented Tommy. "Come pay time, Saturday afternoon, you just couldn't get at him—simply wasn't any way. I was a bit too good for him once, though," remembered Tommy, with a touch of pride in her voice; "got half a quid out of him that time. It did surprise him."

"No," communed Peter to himself aloud, "I don't honestly think there can be any method, creditable or discreditable, that I haven't tried." Peter flung the one-sided interview into the wastepaper-basket, and slipping his notebook into his pocket, departed to drink tea with a lady novelist, whose great desire, as stated in a postscript to her invitation, was to avoid publicity, if possible.

Tommy, as soon as Peter's back was turned, fished it out again.

An hour later in the fog around St. James's Palace stood an Imp, clad in patched trousers and a pepper-and-salt jacket turned up about the neck, gazing with admiring eyes upon the sentry.

"Now, then, young seventeen-and-sixpence the soot," said the sentry, "what do you want?"

"Makes you a bit anxious, don't it," suggested the Imp, "having a big pot like him to look after?"

"Does get a bit on yer mind, if yer thinks about it," agreed the sentry.

"How do you find him to talk to, like?"

"Well," said the sentry, bringing his right leg into action for the purpose of relieving his left, "ain't 'ad much to do with 'im myself, not person'ly, as yet. Oh, 'e ain't a bad sort when yer know 'im."

"That's his shake-down, ain't it?" asked the Imp, "where the lights are."

"That's it," admitted sentry. "You ain't an Anarchist? Tell me if you are."

"I'll let you know if I feel it coming on," the Imp assured him.

Had the sentry been a man of swift and penetrating observation—which he wasn't—he might have asked the question in more serious a tone. For he would have remarked that the Imp's black eyes were resting lovingly upon a rain-water-pipe, giving to a skilful climber easy access to the terrace underneath the Prince's windows.

"I would like to see him," said the Imp.

"Friend o' yours?" asked the sentry.

"Well, not exactly," admitted the Imp. "But there, you know, everybody's talking about him down our street."

"Well, yer'll 'ave to be quick about it," said the sentry. "'E's off to-night."

Tommy's face fell. "I thought it wasn't till Friday morning."

"Ah!" said the sentry, "that's what the papers say, is it?" The sentry's voice took unconsciously the accent of those from whom no secret is hid. "I'll tell yer what yer can do," continued the sentry, enjoying an unaccustomed sense of importance. The sentry glanced left, then right. "'E's a slipping off all by 'imself down to Osborne by the 6.40 from Waterloo. Nobody knows it—'cept, o' course, just a few of us. That's 'is way all over. 'E just 'ates—"

A footstep sounded down the corridor. The sentry became statuesque.

At Waterloo, Tommy inspected the 6.40 train. Only one compartment indicated possibilities, an extra large one at the end of the coach next the guard's van. It was labelled "Reserved," and in the place of the usual fittings was furnished with a table and four easy-chairs. Having noticed its position, Tommy took a walk up the platform and disappeared into the fog.

Twenty minutes later, Prince Blank stepped hurriedly across the platform, unnoticed save by half a dozen obsequious officials, and entered the compartment reserved for him. The obsequious officials bowed. Prince Blank, in military fashion, raised his hand. The 6.40 steamed out slowly.

Prince Blank, who was a stout gentleman, though he tried to disguise the fact, seldom found himself alone. When he did, he generally indulged himself in a little healthy relaxation. With two hours' run to Southampton before him, free from all possibility of intrusion, Prince Blank let loose the buttons of his powerfully built waistcoat, rested his bald head on the top of his chair, stretched his great legs across another, and closed his terrible, small eyes.

For an instant it seemed to Prince Blank that a draught had entered into the carriage. As, however, the sensation immediately passed away, he did not trouble to wake up. Then the Prince dreamed that somebody was in the carriage with him—was sitting opposite to him. This being an annoying sort of dream, the Prince opened his eyes for the purpose of dispelling it. There was somebody sitting opposite to him—a very grimy little person, wiping blood off its face and hands with a dingy handkerchief. Had the Prince been a man capable of surprise, he would have been surprised.

"It's all right," assured him Tommy. "I ain't here to do any harm. I ain't an Anarchist."

The Prince, by a muscular effort, retired some four or five inches and commenced to rebutton his waistcoat.

"How did you get here?" asked the Prince.

"'Twas a bigger job than I'd reckoned on," admitted Tommy, seeking a dry inch in the smeared handkerchief, and finding none. "But that don't matter," added Tommy cheerfully, "now I'm here."

"If you do not wish me to hand you over to the police at Southampton, you had better answer my questions," remarked the Prince drily.

Tommy was not afraid of princes, but in the lexicon of her harassed youth "Police" had always been a word of dread.

"I wanted to get at you."

"I gather that."

"There didn't seem any other way. It's jolly difficult to get at you. You're so jolly artful."

"Tell me how you managed it."

"There's a little bridge for signals just outside Waterloo. I could see that the train would have to pass under it. So I climbed up and waited. It being a foggy night, you see, nobody twigged me. I say, you are Prince Blank, ain't you?"

"I am Prince Blank."

"Should have been mad if I'd landed the wrong man."

"Go on."

"I knew which was your carriage—leastways, I guessed it; and as it came along, I did a drop." Tommy spread out her arms and legs to illustrate the action. "The lamps, you know," explained Tommy, still dabbing at her face—"one of them caught me."

"And from the roof?"

"Oh, well, it was easy after that. There's an iron thing at the back, and steps. You've only got to walk downstairs and round the corner, and there you are. Bit of luck your other door not being locked. I hadn't thought of that. Haven't got such a thing as a handkerchief about you, have you?"

The Prince drew one from his sleeve and passed it to her. "You mean to tell me, boy—"

"Ain't a boy," explained Tommy. "I'm a girl!"

She said it sadly. Deeming her new friends such as could be trusted, Tommy had accepted their statement that she really was a girl. But for many a long year to come the thought of her lost manhood tinged her voice with bitterness.

"A girl!"

Tommy nodded her head.

"Umph!" said the Prince; "I have heard a good deal about the English girl. I was beginning to think it exaggerated. Stand up."

Tommy obeyed. It was not altogether her way; but with those eyes beneath their shaggy brows bent upon her, it seemed the simplest thing to do.

"So. And now that you are here, what do you want?"

"To interview you."

Tommy drew forth her list of questions.

The shaggy brows contracted.

"Who put you up to this absurdity? Who was it? Tell me at once."

"Nobody."

"Don't lie to me. His name?"

The terrible, small eyes flashed fire. But Tommy also had a pair of eyes. Before their blaze of indignation the great man positively quailed. This type of opponent was new to him.

"I'm not lying."

"I beg your pardon," said the Prince.

And at this point it occurred to the Prince, who being really a great man, had naturally a sense of humour, that a conference conducted on these lines between the leading statesman of an Empire and an impertinent hussy of, say, twelve years old at the outside, might end by becoming ridiculous. So the Prince took up his chair and put it down again beside Tommy's, and employing skilfully his undoubted diplomatic gifts, drew from her bit by bit the whole story.

"I'm inclined, Miss Jane," said the Great Man, the story ended, "to agree with our friend Mr. Hope. I should say your *metier* was journalism."

"And you'll let me interview you?" asked Tommy, showing her white teeth.

The Great Man, laying a hand heavier than he guessed on Tommy's shoulder, rose. "I think you are entitled to it."

"What's your views?" demanded Tommy, reading, "of the future political and social relationships—"

"Perhaps," suggested the Great Man, "it will be simpler if I write it myself."

"Well," concurred Tommy; "my spelling is a bit rocky."

The Great Man drew a chair to the table.

"You won't miss out anything—will you?" insisted Tommy.

"I shall endeavour, Miss Jane, to give you no cause for complaint," gravely he assured her, and sat down to write.

Not till the train began to slacken speed had the Prince finished. Then, blotting and refolding the paper, he stood up.

"I have added some instructions on the back of the last page," explained the Prince, "to which you will draw Mr. Hope's particular attention. I would wish you to promise me, Miss Jane, never again to have recourse to dangerous acrobatic tricks, not even in the sacred cause of journalism."

"Of course, if you hadn't been so jolly difficult to get at—"

"My fault, I know," agreed the Prince. "There is not the least doubt as to which sex you belong to. Nevertheless, I want you to promise me. Come," urged the Prince, "I have done a good deal for you—more than you know."

"All right," consented Tommy a little sulkily. Tommy hated making promises, because she always kept them. "I promise."

"There is your Interview." The first Southampton platform lamp shone in upon the Prince and Tommy as they stood facing one another. The Prince, who had acquired the reputation, not altogether unjustly, of an ill-tempered and savage old gentleman, did a strange thing: taking the little, blood-smeared face between his paws, he kissed it. Tommy always remembered the smoky flavour of the bristly grey moustache.

"One thing more," said the Prince sternly—"not a word of all this. Don't open your mouth to speak of it till you are back in Gough Square."

"Do you take me for a mug?" answered Tommy.

They behaved very oddly to Tommy after the Prince had disappeared. Everybody took a deal of trouble for her, but none of them seemed to know why they were doing it. They looked at her and went away, and came again and looked at her. And the more they thought about it, the more puzzled they became. Some of them asked her questions, but what Tommy really didn't know, added to what she didn't mean to tell, was so prodigious that Curiosity itself paled at contemplation of it.

They washed and brushed her up and gave her an excellent supper; and putting her into a first-class compartment labelled "Reserved," sent her back to Waterloo, and thence in a cab to Gough Square, where she arrived about midnight, suffering from a sense of self-importance, traces of which to this day are still discernible.

Such and thus was the beginning of all things. Tommy, having talked for half an hour at the rate of two hundred words a minute, had suddenly dropped her head upon the table, had been aroused with difficulty and persuaded to go to bed. Peter, in the deep easy-chair before the fire, sat long into the night. Elizabeth, liking quiet company, purred softly. Out of the shadows crept to Peter Hope an old forgotten dream—the dream of a wonderful new Journal, price one penny weekly, of which the Editor should come to be one Thomas Hope, son of Peter Hope, its honoured Founder and Originator: a powerful Journal that should supply a long-felt want, popular, but at the same time elevating—a pleasure to the public, a profit to its owners. "Do you not remember me?" whispered the Dream. "We had long talks together. The morning and the noonday pass. The evening still is ours. The twilight also brings its promise."

Elizabeth stopped purring and looked up surprised. Peter was laughing to himself.

STORY THE SECOND

William Clodd Appoints Himself Managing Director

M RS. POSTWHISTLE sat on a Windsor-chair in the centre of Rolls Court. Mrs. Postwhistle, who, in the days of
her Hebehood, had been likened by admiring frequenters
of the old Mitre in Chancery Lane to the ladies, somewhat emaci-
ated, that an English artist, since become famous, was then com-
mencing to popularise, had developed with the passing years, yet
still retained a face of placid youthfulness. The two facts, taken
in conjunction, had resulted in an asset to her income not to be
despised. The wanderer through Rolls Court this summer's afternoon, presuming him to be familiar with current journalism, would
have retired haunted by the sense that the restful-looking lady on
the Windsor-chair was someone that he ought to know. Glancing
through almost any illustrated paper of the period, the problem
would have been solved for him. A photograph of Mrs. Postwhistle,
taken quite recently, he would have encountered with this legend:
"*Before* use of Professor Hardtop's certain cure for corpulency." Beside it a photograph of Mrs. Postwhistle, then Arabella Higgins,
taken twenty years ago, the legend slightly varied: "*After* use," etc.
The face was the same, the figure—there was no denying it—had
undergone decided alteration.

Mrs. Postwhistle had reached with her chair the centre of Rolls
Court in course of following the sun. The little shop, over the
lintel of which ran: "Timothy Postwhistle, Grocer and Provision

Merchant," she had left behind her in the shadow. Old inhabitants of St. Dunstan-in-the-West retained recollection of a gentlemanly figure, always in a very gorgeous waistcoat, with Dundreary whiskers, to be seen occasionally there behind the counter. All customers it would refer, with the air of a Lord High Chamberlain introducing *debutantes*, to Mrs. Postwhistle, evidently regarding itself purely as ornamental. For the last ten years, however, no one had noticed it there, and Mrs. Postwhistle had a facility amounting almost to genius for ignoring or misunderstanding questions it was not to her taste to answer. Most things were suspected, nothing known. St. Dunstan-in-the-West had turned to other problems.

"If I wasn't wanting to see 'im," remarked to herself Mrs. Postwhistle, who was knitting with one eye upon the shop, "'e'd a been 'ere 'fore I'd 'ad time to clear the dinner things away; certain to 'ave been. It's a strange world."

Mrs. Postwhistle was desirous for the arrival of a gentleman not usually awaited with impatience by the ladies of Rolls Court—to wit, one William Clodd, rent-collector, whose day for St. Dunstan-in-the-West was Tuesday.

"At last," said Mrs. Postwhistle, though without hope that Mr. Clodd, who had just appeared at the other end of the court, could possibly hear her. "Was beginning to be afraid as you'd tumbled over yerself in your 'urry and 'urt yerself."

Mr. Clodd, perceiving Mrs. Postwhistle, decided to abandon method and take No. 7 first.

Mr. Clodd was a short, thick-set, bullet-headed young man, with ways that were bustling, and eyes that, though kind, suggested trickiness.

"Ah!" said Mr. Clodd admiringly, as he pocketed the six half-crowns that the lady handed up to him. "If only they were all like you, Mrs. Postwhistle!"

"Wouldn't be no need of chaps like you to worry 'em," pointed out Mrs. Postwhistle.

"It's an irony of fate, my being a rent-collector, when you come to think of it," remarked Mr. Clodd, writing out the receipt. "If I had my way, I'd put an end to landlordism, root and branch. Curse of the country."

"Just the very thing I wanted to talk to you about," returned the lady—"that lodger o' mine."

"Ah! don't pay, don't he? You just hand him over to me. I'll soon have it out of him."

"It's not that," explained Mrs. Postwhistle. "If a Saturday morning 'appened to come round as 'e didn't pay up without me asking, I should know I'd made a mistake—that it must be Friday. If I don't 'appen to be in at 'alf-past ten, 'e puts it in an envelope and leaves it on the table."

"Wonder if his mother has got any more like him?" mused Mr. Clodd. "Could do with a few about this neighbourhood. What is it you want to say about him, then? Merely to brag about him?"

"I wanted to ask you," continued Mrs. Postwhistle, "'ow I could get rid of 'im. It was rather a curious agreement."

"Why do you want to get rid of him? Too noisy?"

"Noisy! Why, the cat makes more noise about the 'ouse than 'e does. 'E'd make 'is fortune as a burglar."

"Come home late?"

"Never known 'im out after the shutters are up."

"Gives you too much trouble then?"

"I can't say that of 'im. Never know whether 'e's in the 'ouse or isn't, without going upstairs and knocking at the door."

"Here, you tell it your own way," suggested the bewildered Clodd. "If it was anyone else but you, I should say you didn't know your own business."

"'E gets on my nerves," said Mrs. Postwhistle. "You ain't in a 'urry for five minutes?"

Mr. Clodd was always in a hurry. "But I can forget it talking to you," added the gallant Mr. Clodd.

Mrs. Postwhistle led the way into the little parlour.

"Just the name of it," consented Mr. Clodd. "Cheerfulness combined with temperance; that's the ideal."

"I'll tell you what 'appened only last night," commenced Mrs. Postwhistle, seating herself the opposite side of the loo-table. "A letter came for 'im by the seven o'clock post. I'd seen 'im go out two hours before, and though I'd been sitting in the shop the whole blessed time, I never saw or 'eard 'im pass through. E's like that. It's like 'aving a ghost for a lodger. I opened 'is door without knocking and went in. If you'll believe me, 'e was clinging with 'is arms and legs to the top of the bedstead—it's one of those old-fashioned, four-post things—'is 'ead touching the ceiling. 'E 'adn't got too much

29

clothes on, and was cracking nuts with 'is teeth and eating 'em. 'E threw a 'andful of shells at me, and making the most awful faces at me, started off gibbering softly to himself."

"All play, I suppose? No real vice?" commented the interested Mr. Clodd.

"It will go on for a week, that will," continued Mrs. Postwhistle—"'e fancying 'imself a monkey. Last week he was a tortoise, and was crawling about on his stomach with a tea-tray tied on to 'is back. 'E's as sensible as most men, if that's saying much, the moment 'e's outside the front door; but in the 'ouse—well, I suppose the fact is that 'e's a lunatic."

"Don't seem no hiding anything from you," Mrs. Postwhistle remarked Mr. Clodd in tones of admiration. "Does he ever get violent?"

"Don't know what 'e would be like if 'e 'appened to fancy 'imself something really dangerous," answered Mrs. Postwhistle. "I am a bit nervous of this new monkey game, I don't mind confessing to you—the things that they do according to the picture-books. Up to now, except for imagining 'imself a mole, and taking all his meals underneath the carpet, it's been mostly birds and cats and 'armless sort o' things I 'aven't seemed to mind so much."

"How did you get hold of him?" demanded Mr. Clodd. "Have much trouble in finding him, or did somebody come and tell you about him?"

"Old Gladman, of Chancery Lane, the law stationer, brought 'im 'ere one evening about two months ago—said 'e was a sort of distant relative of 'is, a bit soft in the 'ead, but perfectly 'armless—wanted to put 'im with someone who wouldn't impose on 'im. Well, what between 'aving been empty for over five weeks, the poor old gaby 'imself looking as gentle as a lamb, and the figure being reasonable, I rather jumped at the idea; and old Gladman, explaining as 'ow 'e wanted the thing settled and done with, got me to sign a letter."

"Kept a copy of it?" asked the business-like Clodd.

"No. But I can remember what it was. Gladman 'ad it all ready. So long as the money was paid punctual and 'e didn't make no disturbance and didn't fall sick, I was to go on boarding and lodging 'im for seventeen-and-sixpence a week. It didn't strike me as anything to be objected to at the time; but 'e payin' regular, as I've explained to you, and be'aving, so far as disturbance is concerned, more like a Christian martyr than a man, well, it looks to me as if I'd got to live and die with 'im."

"Give him rope, and possibly he'll have a week at being a howling hyaena, or a laughing jackass, or something of that sort that will lead to a disturbance," thought Mr. Clodd, "in which case, of course, you would have your remedy."

"Yes," thought Mrs. Postwhistle, "and possibly also 'e may take it into what 'e calls is 'ead to be a tiger or a bull, and then perhaps before 'e's through with it I'll be beyond the reach of remedies."

"Leave it to me," said Mr. Clodd, rising and searching for his hat. "I know old Gladman; I'll have a talk with him."

"You might get a look at that letter if you can," suggested Mrs. Postwhistle, "and tell me what you think about it. I don't want to spend the rest of my days in a lunatic asylum of my own if I can 'elp it."

"You leave it to me," was Mr. Clodd's parting assurance.

The July moon had thrown a silver veil over the grimness of Rolls Court when, five hours later, Mr. Clodd's nailed boots echoed again upon its uneven pavement; but Mr. Clodd had no eye for moon or stars or such-like; always he had things more important to think of.

"Seen the old 'umbug?" asked Mrs. Postwhistle, who was partial to the air, leading the way into the parlour.

"First and foremost commenced," Mr. Clodd, as he laid aside his hat, "it is quite understood that you really do want to get rid of him? What's that?" demanded Mr. Clodd, a heavy thud upon the floor above having caused him to start out of his chair.

"'E came in an hour after you'd gone," explained Mrs. Postwhistle, "bringing with him a curtain pole as 'e'd picked up for a shilling in Clare Market. 'E's rested one end upon the mantelpiece and tied the other to the back of the easy-chair—'is idea is to twine 'imself round it and go to sleep upon it. Yes, you've got it quite right without a single blunder. I do want to get rid of 'im."

"Then," said Mr. Clodd, reseating himself, "it can be done."

"Thank God for that!" was Mrs. Postwhistle's pious ejaculation.

"It is just as I thought," continued Mr. Clodd. "The old innocent—he's Gladman's brother-in-law, by the way—has got a small annuity. I couldn't get the actual figure, but I guess it's about sufficient pay for his keep and leave old Gladman, who is running him, a very decent profit. They don't want to send him to an asylum. They can't say he's a pauper, and to put him into a private establishment would swallow up, most likely, the whole of his income. On the other hand, they don't want the bother of looking after him themselves. I talked pretty straight to the old man—let him see I understood the business; and—well, to cut a long story short, I'm willing to take on the job, provided you really want to have done with it, and Gladman is willing in that case to let you off your contract."

Mrs. Postwhistle went to the cupboard to get Mr. Clodd a drink. Another thud upon the floor above—one suggestive of exceptional velocity—arrived at the precise moment when Mrs. Postwhistle, the tumbler level with her eye, was in the act of measuring.

"I call this making a disturbance," said Mrs. Postwhistle, regarding the broken fragments.

"It's only for another night," comforted her Mr. Clodd. "I'll take him away some time to-morrow. Meanwhile, if I were you, I should spread a mattress underneath that perch of his before I went to bed. I should like him handed over to me in reasonable repair."

"It will deaden the sound a bit, any'ow," agreed Mrs. Postwhistle.

"Success to temperance," drank Mr. Clodd, and rose to go.

"I take it you've fixed things up all right for yourself," said Mrs. Postwhistle; "and nobody can blame you if you 'ave. 'Eaven bless you, is what I say."

"We shall get on together," prophesied Mr. Clodd. "I'm fond of animals."

Early the next morning a four-wheeled cab drew up at the entrance to Rolls Court, and in it and upon it went away Clodd and Clodd's Lunatic (as afterwards he came to be known), together with all the belongings of Clodd's Lunatic, the curtain-pole included; and there appeared again behind the fanlight of the little grocer's shop the intimation: "Lodgings for a Single Man," which caught the eye a few days later of a weird-looking, lanky, rawboned laddie, whose language Mrs. Postwhistle found difficulty for a time in comprehending; and that is why one sometimes meets to-day worshippers of Kail Yard literature wandering disconsolately about St. Dunstan-in-the-West, seeking Rolls Court, discomforted because it is no more. But that is the history of the "Wee Laddie," and this of the beginnings of William Clodd, now Sir William Clodd, Bart., M.P., proprietor of a quarter of a hundred newspapers, magazines, and journals: "Truthful Billy" we called him then.

No one can say of Clodd that he did not deserve whatever profit his unlicensed lunatic asylum may have brought him. A kindly man was William Clodd when indulgence in sentiment did not interfere with business.

"There's no harm in him," asserted Mr. Clodd, talking the matter over with one Mr. Peter Hope, journalist, of Gough Square. "He's just a bit dotty, same as you or I might get with nothing to do and all day long to do it in. Kid's play, that's all it is. The best plan, I find, is to treat it as a game and take a hand in it. Last week he wanted to be a lion. I could see that was going to be awkward, he roaring for raw meat and thinking to prowl about the house at night. Well, I didn't nag him—that's no good. I just got a gun and shot him. He's a duck now, and I'm trying to keep him one: sits for an hour beside his bath on three china eggs I've bought him. Wish some of the sane ones were as little trouble."

The summer came again. Clodd and his Lunatic, a mild-looking little old gentleman of somewhat clerical cut, one often met with arm-in-arm, bustling about the streets and courts that were the scene of Clodd's rent-collecting labours. Their evident attachment to one another was curiously displayed; Clodd, the young and red-haired, treating his white-haired, withered companion with fatherly indulgence; the other glancing up from time to time into Clodd's face with a winning expression of infantile affection.

"We are getting much better," explained Clodd, the pair meeting Peter Hope one day at the corner of Newcastle Street. "The more we are out in the open air, and the more we have to do and think about, the better for us—eh?"

The mild-looking little old gentleman hanging on Clodd's arm smiled and nodded.

"Between ourselves," added Mr. Clodd, sinking his voice, "we are not half as foolish as folks think we are."

Peter Hope went his way down the Strand.

"Clodd's a good sort—a good sort," said Peter Hope, who, having in his time lived much alone, had fallen into the habit of speaking his thoughts aloud; "but he's not the man to waste his time. I wonder."

With the winter Clodd's Lunatic fell ill.

Clodd bustled round to Chancery Lane.

"To tell you the truth," confessed Mr. Gladman, "we never thought he would live so long as he has."

"There's the annuity you've got to think of," said Clodd, whom his admirers of to-day (and they are many, for he must be a millionaire by this time) are fond of alluding to as "that frank, outspoken Englishman." "Wouldn't it be worth your while to try what taking him away from the fogs might do for him?"

Old Gladman seemed inclined to consider the question, but Mrs. Gladman, a brisk, cheerful little woman, had made up her mind.

"We've had what there is to have," said Mrs. Gladman. "He's seventy-three. What's the sense of risking good money? Be content."

No one could say—no one ever did say—that Clodd, under the circumstances, did not do his best. Perhaps, after all, nothing could have helped. The little old gentleman, at Clodd's suggestion, played at being a dormouse and lay very still. If he grew restless, thereby bringing on his cough, Clodd, as a terrible black cat, was watching to pounce upon him. Only by keeping very quiet and artfully pretending to be asleep could he hope to escape the ruthless Clodd.

Doctor William Smith (ne Wilhelm Schmidt) shrugged his fat shoulders. "We can do noding. Dese fogs of ours: id is de one ting dat enables the foreigner to crow over us. Keep him quiet. De dormouse—id is a goot idea."

That evening William Clodd mounted to the second floor of 16, Gough Square, where dwelt his friend, Peter Hope, and knocked briskly at the door.

"Come in," said a decided voice, which was not Peter Hope's.

Mr. William Clodd's ambition was, and always had been, to be the owner or part-owner of a paper. To-day, as I have said, he owns a quarter of a hundred, and is in negotiation, so rumour goes, for seven more. But twenty years ago "Clodd and Co., Limited," was but in embryo. And Peter Hope, journalist, had likewise and for many a long year cherished the ambition to be, before he died, the owner or part-owner of a paper. Peter Hope to-day owns nothing, except perhaps the knowledge, if such things be permitted, that whenever and wherever his name is mentioned, kind thoughts arise unbidden—that someone of the party will surely say: "Dear old Peter! What a good fellow he was!" Which also may be in its way a valuable possession: who knows? But twenty years ago Peter's horizon was limited by Fleet Street.

Peter Hope was forty-seven, so he said, a dreamer and a scholar. William Clodd was three-and-twenty, a born hustler, very wide

awake. Meeting one day by accident upon an omnibus, when Clodd
lent Peter, who had come out without his purse, threepence to
pay his fare with; drifting into acquaintanceship, each had come
to acquire a liking and respect for the other. The dreamer thought
with wonder of Clodd's shrewd practicability; the cute young man
of business was lost in admiration of what seemed to him his old
friend's marvellous learning. Both had arrived at the conclusion that
a weekly journal with Peter Hope as editor, and William Clodd as
manager, would be bound to be successful.

"If only we could scrape together a thousand pounds!" had
sighed Peter.

"The moment we lay our hands upon the coin, we'll start that
paper. Remember, it's a bargain," had answered William Clodd.

Mr. William Clodd turned the handle and walked in. With the
door still in his hand he paused to look round the room. It was the
first time he had seen it. His meetings hitherto with Peter Hope had
been chance *rencontres* in street or restaurant. Always had he been
curious to view the sanctuary of so much erudition.

A large, oak-panelled room, its three high windows, each with a
low, cushioned seat beneath it, giving on to Gough Square. Thirty-
five years before, Peter Hope, then a young dandy with side whiskers close-cropped and terminating just below the ear; with wavy,
brown hair, giving to his fresh-complexioned face an appearance
almost girlish; in cut-away blue coat, flowered waistcoat, black
silk cravat secured by two gold pins chained together, and tightly
strapped grey trouserings, had, aided and abetted by a fragile little
lady in crinoline and much-flounced skirt, and bodice somewhat
low, with corkscrew curls each movement of her head set ringing,
planned and furnished it in accordance with the sober canons then
in vogue, spending thereupon more than they should, as is to be
expected from the young to whom the future promises all things.
The fine Brussels carpet! A little too bright, had thought the shaking curls. "The colours will tone down, miss—ma'am." The shopman knew. Only by the help of the round island underneath the
massive Empire table, by excursions into untrodden corners, could
Peter recollect the rainbow floor his feet had pressed when he was
twenty-one. The noble bookcase, surmounted by Minerva's bust.
Really it was too expensive. But the nodding curls had been so obstinate. Peter's silly books and papers must be put away in order;

the curls did not intend to permit any excuse for untidiness. So, too, the handsome, brass-bound desk; it must be worthy of the beautiful thoughts Peter would pen upon it. The great sideboard, supported by two such angry-looking mahogany lions; it must be strong to support the weight of silver clever Peter would one day purchase to place upon it. The few oil paintings in their heavy frames. A solidly furnished, sober apartment; about it that subtle atmosphere of dignity one finds but in old rooms long undisturbed, where one seems to read upon the walls: "I, Joy and Sorrow, twain in one, have dwelt here." One item only there was that seemed out of place among its grave surroundings—a guitar, hanging from the wall, ornamented with a ridiculous blue bow, somewhat faded.

"Mr. William Clodd?" demanded the decided voice.

Clodd started and closed the door.

"Guessed it in once," admitted Mr. Clodd.

"I thought so," said the decided voice. "We got your note this afternoon. Mr. Hope will be back at eight. Will you kindly hang up your hat and coat in the hall? You will find a box of cigars on the mantelpiece. Excuse my being busy. I must finish this, then I'll talk to you."

The owner of the decided voice went on writing. Clodd, having done as he was bid, sat himself in the easy-chair before the fire and smoked. Of the person behind the desk Mr. Clodd could see but the head and shoulders. It had black, curly hair, cut short. It's only garment visible below the white collar and red tie might have been a boy's jacket designed more like a girl's, or a girl's designed more like a boy's; partaking of the genius of English statesmanship, it appeared to be a compromise. Mr. Clodd remarked the long, drooping lashes over the bright, black eyes.

"It's a girl," said Mr. Clodd to himself; "rather a pretty girl."

Mr. Clodd, continuing downward, arrived at the nose.

"No," said Mr. Clodd to himself, "it's a boy—a cheeky young beggar, I should say."

The person at the desk, giving a grunt of satisfaction, gathered together sheets of manuscript and arranged them; then, resting its elbows on the desk and taking its head between its hands, regarded Mr. Clodd.

"Don't you hurry yourself," said Mr. Clodd; "but when you really have finished, tell me what you think of me."

"I beg your pardon," apologised the person at the desk. "I have got into a habit of staring at people. I know it's rude. I'm trying to break myself of it."

"Tell me your name," suggested Mr. Clodd, "and I'll forgive you."

"Tommy," was the answer—"I mean Jane."

"Make up your mind," advised Mr. Clodd; "don't let me influence you. I only want the truth."

"You see," explained the person at the desk, "everybody calls me Tommy, because that used to be my name. But now it's Jane."

"I see," said Mr. Clodd. "And which am I to call you?"

The person at the desk pondered. "Well, if this scheme you and Mr. Hope have been talking about really comes to anything, we shall be a good deal thrown together, you see, and then I expect you'll call me Tommy—most people do."

"You've heard about the scheme? Mr. Hope has told you?"

"Why, of course," replied Tommy. "I'm Mr. Hope's devil."

For the moment Clodd doubted whether his old friend had not started a rival establishment to his own.

"I help him in his work," Tommy relieved his mind by explaining. "In journalistic circles we call it devilling."

"I understand," said Mr. Clodd. "And what do you think, Tommy, of the scheme? I may as well start calling you Tommy, because, between you and me, I think the idea will come to something."

Tommy fixed her black eyes upon him. She seemed to be looking him right through.

"You are staring again, Tommy," Clodd reminded her. "You'll have trouble breaking yourself of that habit, I can see."

"I was trying to make up my mind about you. Everything depends upon the business man."

"Glad to hear you say so," replied the self-satisfied Clodd.

"If you are very clever—Do you mind coming nearer to the lamp? I can't quite see you over there."

Clodd never could understand why he did it—never could understand why, from first to last, he always did what Tommy wished him to do; his only consolation being that other folks seemed just as helpless. He rose and, crossing the long room, stood at attention before the large desk, nervousness, to which he was somewhat of a stranger, taking possession of him.

"You don't *look* very clever."

Clodd experienced another new sensation—that of falling in his own estimation.

"And yet one can see that you *are* clever."

The mercury of Clodd's conceit shot upward to a point that in the case of anyone less physically robust might have been dangerous to health.

Clodd held out his hand. "We'll pull it through, Tommy. The Guv'nor shall find the literature; you and I will make it go. I like you."

And Peter Hope, entering at the moment, caught a spark from the light that shone in the eyes of William Clodd and Tommy, whose other name was Jane, as, gripping hands, they stood with the desk between them, laughing they knew not why. And the years fell from old Peter, and, again a boy, he also laughed he knew not why. He had sipped from the wine-cup of youth.

"It's all settled, Guv'nor!" cried Clodd. "Tommy and I have fixed things up. We'll start with the New Year."

"You've got the money?"

"I'm reckoning on it. I don't see very well how I can miss it."

"Sufficient?"

"Just about. You get to work."

"I've saved a little," began Peter. "It ought to have been more, but somehow it isn't."

"Perhaps we shall want it," Clodd replied; "perhaps we shan't. You are supplying the brains."

The three for a few moments remained silent.

"I think, Tommy," said Peter, "I think a bottle of the old Madeira—"

"Not to-night," said Clodd; "next time."

"To drink success," urged Peter.

"One man's success generally means some other poor devil's misfortune," answered Clodd.

"Can't be helped, of course, but don't want to think about it to-night. Must be getting back to my dormouse. Good night."

Clodd shook hands and bustled out.

"I thought as much," mused Peter aloud.

"What an odd mixture the man is! Kind—no one could have been kinder to the poor old fellow. Yet all the while—We are an odd mixture, Tommy," said Peter Hope, "an odd mixture, we men and women." Peter was a philosopher.

The white-whiskered old dormouse soon coughed himself to sleep for ever.

"I shall want you and the missis to come to the funeral, Gladman," said Mr. Clodd, as he swung into the stationer's shop; "and bring Pincer with you. I'm writing to him."

"Don't see what good we can do," demurred Gladman.

"Well, you three are his only relatives; it's only decent you should be present," urged Clodd. "Besides, there's the will to be read. You may care to hear it."

The dry old law stationer opened wide his watery eyes.

"His will! Why, what had he got to leave? There was nothing but the annuity."

"You turn up at the funeral," Clodd told him, "and you'll learn all about it. Bonner's clerk will be there and will bring it with him. Everything is going to be done *comme il faut*, as the French say."

"I ought to have known of this," began Mr. Gladman.

"Glad to find you taking so much interest in the old chap," said Clodd. "Pity he's dead and can't thank you."

"I warn you," shouted old Gladman, whose voice was rising to a scream, "he was a helpless imbecile, incapable of acting for himself! If any undue influence—"

"See you on Friday," broke in Clodd, who was busy.

Friday's ceremony was not a sociable affair. Mrs. Gladman spoke occasionally in a shrill whisper to Mr. Gladman, who replied with grunts. Both employed the remainder of their time in scowling at Clodd. Mr. Pincer, a stout, heavy gentleman connected with the House of Commons, maintained a ministerial reserve. The undertaker's foreman expressed himself as thankful when it was over. He criticised it as the humpiest funeral he had ever known; for a time he had serious thoughts of changing his profession.

The solicitor's clerk was waiting for the party on its return from Kensal Green. Clodd again offered hospitality. Mr. Pincer this time allowed himself a glass of weak whisky-and-water, and sipped it with an air of doing so without prejudice. The clerk had one a little stronger, Mrs. Gladman, dispensing with consultation, declined shrilly for self and partner. Clodd, explaining that he always followed legal precedent, mixed himself one also and drank "To our next happy meeting." Then the clerk read.

It was a short and simple will, dated the previous August. It appeared that the old gentleman, unknown to his relatives, had died possessed of shares in a silver mine, once despaired of, now prospering. Taking them at present value, they would produce a sum well over two thousand pounds. The old gentleman had bequeathed five hundred pounds to his brother-in-law, Mr. Gladman; five hundred pounds to his only other living relative, his first cousin, Mr. Pincer; the residue to his friend, William Clodd, as a return for the many kindnesses that gentleman had shown him.

Mr. Gladman rose, more amused than angry.

"And you think you are going to pocket that one thousand to twelve hundred pounds. You really do?" he asked Mr. Clodd, who, with legs stretched out before him, sat with his hands deep in his trousers pockets.

"That's the idea," admitted Mr. Clodd.

Mr. Gladman laughed, but without much lightening the atmosphere. "Upon my word, Clodd, you amuse me—you quite amuse me," repeated Mr. Gladman.

"You always had a sense of humour," commented Mr. Clodd.

"You villain! You double-dyed villain!" screamed Mr. Gladman, suddenly changing his tone. "You think the law is going to allow you to swindle honest men! You think we are going to sit still for you to rob us! That will—" Mr. Gladman pointed a lank forefinger dramatically towards the table.

"You mean to dispute it?" inquired Mr. Clodd.

For a moment Mr. Gladman stood aghast at the other's coolness, but soon found his voice again.

"Dispute it!" he shrieked. "Do you dispute that you influenced him?—dictated it to him word for word, made the poor old helpless idiot sign it, he utterly incapable of even understanding—"

"Don't chatter so much," interrupted Mr. Clodd. "It's not a pretty voice, yours. What I asked you was, do you intend to dispute it?"

"If you will kindly excuse us," struck in Mrs. Gladman, addressing Mr. Clodd with an air of much politeness, "we shall just have time, if we go now, to catch our solicitor before he leaves his office."

Mr. Gladman took up his hat from underneath his chair.

"One moment," suggested Mr. Clodd. "I did influence him to make that will. If you don't like it, there's an end of it."

"Of course," commenced Mr. Gladman in a mollified tone.

"Sit down," suggested Mr. Clodd. "Let's try another one." Mr. Clodd turned to the clerk. "The previous one, Mr. Wright, if you please; the one dated June the 10th."

An equally short and simple document, it bequeathed three hundred pounds to Mr. William Clodd in acknowledgment of kindnesses received, the residue to the Royal Zoological Society of London, the deceased having been always interested in and fond of animals. The relatives, "Who have never shown me the slightest affection or given themselves the slightest trouble concerning me, and who have already received considerable sums out of my income," being by name excluded.

"I may mention," observed Mr. Clodd, no one else appearing inclined to break the silence, "that in suggesting the Royal Zoological Society to my poor old friend as a fitting object for his benevolence, I had in mind a very similar case that occurred five years ago. A bequest to them was disputed on the grounds that the testator was of unsound mind. They had to take their case to the House of Lords before they finally won it."

"Anyhow," remarked Mr. Gladman, licking his lips, which were dry, "you won't get anything, Mr. Clodd—no, not even your three-hundred pounds, clever as you think yourself. My brother-in-law's money will go to the lawyers."

Then Mr. Pincer rose and spoke slowly and clearly. "If there must be a lunatic connected with our family, which I don't see why there should be, it seems to me to be you, Nathaniel Gladman."

Mr. Gladman stared back with open mouth. Mr. Pincer went on impressively.

"As for my poor old cousin Joe, he had his eccentricities, but that was all. I for one am prepared to swear that he was of sound mind in August last and quite capable of making his own will. It seems to me that the other thing, dated in June, is just waste paper."

Mr. Pincer having delivered himself, sat down again. Mr. Gladman showed signs of returning language.

"Oh! what's the use of quarrelling?" chirped in cheery Mrs. Gladman. "It's five hundred pounds we never expected. Live and let live is what I always say."

"It's the damned artfulness of the thing," said Mr. Gladman, still very white about the gills.

"Oh, you have a little something to thaw your face," suggested his wife.

Mr. and Mrs. Gladman, on the strength of the five hundred pounds, went home in a cab. Mr. Pincer stayed behind and made a night of it with Mr. Clodd and Bonner's clerk, at Clodd's expense.

The residue worked out at eleven hundred and sixty-nine pounds and a few shillings. The capital of the new company, "established for the purpose of carrying on the business of newspaper publishers and distributors, printers, advertising agents, and any other trade and enterprise affiliated to the same," was one thousand pounds in one pound shares, fully paid up; of which William Clodd, Esquire, was registered proprietor of four hundred and sixty-three; Peter Hope, M.A., of 16, Gough Square, of also four hundred and sixty-three; Miss Jane Hope, adopted daughter of said Peter Hope (her real name nobody, herself included, ever having known), and generally called Tommy, of three, paid for by herself after a battle royal with William Clodd; Mrs. Postwhistle, of Rolls Court, of ten, presented by the promoter; Mr. Pincer, of the House of Commons, also of ten (still owing for); Dr. Smith (ne Schmidt) of fifty; James Douglas Alexander Calder McTear (otherwise the "Wee Laddie"), residing then in Mrs. Postwhistle's first floor front, of one, paid for by poem published in the first number: "The Song of the Pen."

Choosing a title for the paper cost much thought. Driven to despair, they called it *Good Humour.*

STORY THE THIRD

Grindley Junior Drops into the Position of Publisher

EW are the ways of the West Central district that have changed less within the last half-century than Nevill's Court, leading from Great New Street into Fetter Lane. Its north side still consists of the same quaint row of small low shops that stood there—doing perhaps a little brisker business—when George the Fourth was King; its southern side of the same three substantial houses each behind a strip of garden, pleasant by contrast with surrounding grimness, built long ago —some say before Queen Anne was dead.

Out of the largest of these, passing through the garden, then well cared for, came one sunny Sunday morning, some fifteen years before the commencement proper of this story, one Solomon Appleyard, pushing in front of him a perambulator. At the brick wall surmounted by wooden railings that divides the garden from the court, Solomon paused, hearing behind him the voice of Mrs. Appleyard speaking from the doorstep.

"If I don't see you again until dinner-time, I'll try and get on without you, understand. Don't think of nothing but your pipe and forget the child. And be careful of the crossings."

Mrs. Appleyard retired into the darkness. Solomon, steering the perambulator carefully, emerged from Nevill's Court without accident. The quiet streets drew Solomon westward. A vacant seat beneath the shade overlooking the Long Water in Kensington Gardens invited to rest.

"Piper?" suggested a small boy to Solomon. "*Sunday Times, 'Server?*"

"My boy," said Mr. Appleyard, speaking slowly, "when you've been mewed up with newspapers eighteen hours a day for six days a week, you can do without 'em for a morning. Take 'em away. I want to forget the smell of 'em."

Solomon, having assured himself that the party in the perambulator was still breathing, crossed his legs and lit his pipe.

"Hezekiah!"

The exclamation had been wrung from Solomon Appleyard by the approach of a stout, short man clad in a remarkably ill-fitting broad-cloth suit.

"What, Sol, my boy?"

"It looked like you," said Solomon. "And then I said to myself: 'No; surely it can't be Hezekiah; he'll be at chapel.'"

"You run about," said Hezekiah, addressing a youth of some four summers he had been leading by the hand. "Don't you go out of my sight; and whatever you do, don't you do injury to those new clothes of yours, or you'll wish you'd never been put into them. The truth is," continued Hezekiah to his friend, his sole surviving son and heir being out of earshot, "the morning tempted me. 'Tain't often I get a bit of fresh air."

"Doing well?"

"The business," replied Hezekiah, "is going up by leaps and bounds—leaps and bounds. But, of course, all that means harder work for me. It's from six in the morning till twelve o'clock at night."

"There's nothing I know of," returned Solomon, who was something of a pessimist, "that's given away free gratis for nothing except misfortune."

"Keeping yourself up to the mark ain't too easy," continued Hezekiah; "and when it comes to other folks! play's all they think of. Talk religion to them—why, they laugh at you! What the world's coming to, I don't know. How's the printing business doing?"

"The printing business," responded the other, removing his pipe and speaking somewhat sadly, "the printing business looks like being a big thing. Capital, of course, is what hampers me—or, rather, the want of it. But Janet, she's careful; she don't waste much, Janet don't."

"Now, with Anne," replied Hezekiah, "it's all the other way—pleasure, gaiety, a day at Rosherville or the Crystal Palace—anything to waste money."

"Ah! she was always fond of her bit of fun," remembered Solomon.

"Fun!" retorted Hezekiah. "I like a bit of fun myself. But not if you've got to pay for it. Where's the fun in that?"

"What I ask myself sometimes," said Solomon, looking straight in front of him, "is what do we do it for?"

"What do we do what for?"

"Work like blessed slaves, depriving ourselves of all enjoyments. What's the sense of it? What—"

A voice from the perambulator beside him broke the thread of Solomon Appleyard's discourse. The sole surviving son of Hezekiah Grindley, seeking distraction and finding none, had crept back unperceived. A perambulator! A thing his experience told him out of which excitement in some form or another could generally be obtained. You worried it and took your chance. Either it howled, in which case you had to run for your life, followed—and, unfortunately, overtaken nine times out of ten—by a whirlwind of vengeance; or it gurgled: in which case the heavens smiled and halos descended on your head. In either event you escaped the deadly ennui that is the result of continuous virtue. Master Grindley, his star having pointed out to him a peacock's feather lying on the ground, had, with one eye upon his unobservant parent, removed the complicated coverings sheltering Miss Helvetia Appleyard from the world, and anticipating by a quarter of a century the prime enjoyment of British youth, had set to work to tickle that lady on the nose. Miss Helvetia Appleyard awakened, did precisely what the tickled British maiden of to-day may be relied upon to do under corresponding circumstances: she first of all took swift and comprehensive survey of the male thing behind the feather. Had he been displeasing in her eyes, she would, one may rely upon it, have anteceded the behaviour in similar case of her descendant of to-day—that is to say, have expressed resentment in no uncertain terms. Master Nathaniel Grindley proving, however, to her taste, that which might have been considered impertinence became accepted as a fit and proper form of introduction. Miss Appleyard smiled graciously—nay, further, intimated desire for more.

"That your only one?" asked the paternal Grindley.

"She's the only one," replied Solomon, speaking in tones less pessimistic.

Miss Appleyard had with the help of Grindley junior wriggled herself into a sitting posture. Grindley junior continued his attentions, the lady indicating by signs the various points at which she was most susceptible.

"Pretty picture they make together, eh?" suggested Hezekiah in a whisper to his friend.

"Never saw her take to anyone like that before," returned Solomon, likewise in a whisper.

A neighbouring church clock chimed twelve. Solomon Appleyard, knocking the ashes from his pipe, arose.

"Don't know any reason myself why we shouldn't see a little more of one another than we do," suggested Grindley senior, shaking hands.

"Give us a look-up one Sunday afternoon," suggested Solomon. "Bring the youngster with you."

Solomon Appleyard and Hezekiah Grindley had started life within a few months of one another some five-and-thirty years before. Likewise within a few hundred yards of one another, Solomon at his father's bookselling and printing establishment on the east side of the High Street of a small Yorkshire town; Hezekiah at his father's grocery shop upon the west side, opposite. Both had married farmers' daughters. Solomon's natural bent towards gaiety Fate had corrected by directing his affections to a partner instinct with Yorkshire shrewdness; and with shrewdness go other qualities that make for success rather than for happiness. Hezekiah, had circumstances been equal, might have been his friend's rival for Janet's capable and saving hand, had not sweet-tempered, laughing Annie Glossop—directed by Providence to her moral welfare, one must presume—fallen in love with him. Between Jane's virtues and Annie's three hundred golden sovereigns Hezekiah had not hesitated a moment. Golden sovereigns were solid facts; wifely virtues, by a serious-minded and strong-willed husband, could be instilled—at all events, light-heartedness suppressed. The two men, Hezekiah urged by his own ambition, Solomon by his wife's, had arrived in London within a year of one another: Hezekiah to open a grocer's shop in Kensington, which those who should have known assured him was a hopeless neighbourhood. But Hezekiah had the instinct of the money-maker. Solomon, after looking about him, had fixed upon the roomy, substantial house in Nevill's Court as a promising foundation for a printer's business.

That was ten years ago. The two friends, scorning delights, living laborious days, had seen but little of one another. Light-hearted Annie had borne to her dour partner two children who had died. Nathaniel George, with the luck supposed to wait on number three, had lived on, and, inheriting fortunately the temperament of his mother, had brought sunshine into the gloomy rooms above the shop in High Street, Kensington. Mrs. Grindley, grown weak and fretful, had rested from her labours.

Mrs. Appleyard's guardian angel, prudent like his protege, had waited till Solomon's business was well established before despatching the stork to Nevill's Court, with a little girl. Later had sent a boy, who, not finding the close air of St. Dunstan to his liking, had found his way back again; thus passing out of this story and all others. And there remained to carry on the legend of the Grindleys and the Appleyards only Nathaniel George, now aged five, and Janet Helvetia, quite a beginner, who took lift seriously.

There are no such things as facts. Narrow-minded folk—surveyors, auctioneers, and such like—would have insisted that the garden between the old Georgian house and Nevill's Court was a strip of land one hundred and eighteen feet by ninety-two, containing a laburnum tree, six laurel bushes, and a dwarf deodora. To Nathaniel George and Janet Helvetia it was the land of Thule, "the furthest boundaries of which no man has reached." On rainy Sunday afternoons they played in the great, gloomy pressroom, where silent ogres, standing motionless, stretched out iron arms to seize them as they ran. Then just when Nathaniel George was eight, and Janet Helvetia four and a half, Hezekiah launched the celebrated "Grindley's Sauce." It added a relish to chops and steaks, transformed cold mutton into a luxury, and swelled the head of Hezekiah Grindley—which was big enough in all conscience as it was—and shrivelled up his little hard heart. The Grindleys and the Appleyards visited no more. As a sensible fellow ought to have seen for himself, so thought Hezekiah, the Sauce had altered all things. The possibility of a marriage between their children, things having remained equal, might have been a pretty fancy; but the son of the great Grindley, whose name in three-foot letters faced the world from every hoarding, would have to look higher than a printer's daughter. Solomon, a sudden and vehement convert to the principles of mediaeval feudalism, would rather see his only child, granddaughter of the author of *The History of Kettlewell* and other works, dead and buried than married to a grocer's son, even though he might inherit a fortune made out of poisoning the public with a mixture of mustard and sour beer. It was many years before Nathaniel George and Janet Helvetia met one another again, and when they did they had forgotten one another.

Hezekiah S. Grindley, a short, stout, and pompous gentleman, sat under a palm in the gorgeously furnished drawing-room of his big house at Notting Hill. Mrs. Grindley, a thin, faded woman, the despair of her dressmaker, sat as near to the fire as its massive and imposing copper outworks would permit, and shivered. Grindley junior, a fair-haired, well-shaped youth, with eyes that the other sex found attractive, leant with his hands in his pockets against a scrupulously robed statue of Diana, and appeared uncomfortable.

"I'm making the money—making it hand over fist. All you'll have to do will be to spend it," Grindley senior was explaining to his son and heir.

"I'll do that all right, dad."

"I'm not so sure of it," was his father's opinion. "You've got to prove yourself worthy to spend it. Don't you think I shall be content to have slaved all these years merely to provide a brainless young idiot with the means of self-indulgence. I leave my money to somebody worthy of me. Understand, sir?—somebody worthy of me."

Mrs. Grindley commenced a sentence; Mr. Grindley turned his small eyes upon her. The sentence remained unfinished.

"You were about to say something," her husband reminded her.

Mrs. Grindley said it was nothing.

"If it is anything worth hearing—if it is anything that will assist the discussion, let's have it." Mr. Grindley waited. "If not, if you yourself do not consider it worth finishing, why have begun it?"

Mr. Grindley returned to his son and heir. "You haven't done too well at school—in fact, your school career has disappointed me."

"I know I'm not clever," Grindley junior offered as an excuse.

"Why not? Why aren't you clever?"

His son and heir was unable to explain.

"You are my son—why aren't you clever? It's laziness, sir; sheer laziness!"

"I'll try and do better at Oxford, sir—honour bright I will!"

"You had better," advised him his father; "because I warn you, your whole future depends upon it. You know me. You've got to be a credit to me, to be worthy of the name of Grindley—or the name, my boy, is all you'll have."

Old Grindley meant it, and his son knew that he meant it. The old Puritan principles and instincts were strong in the old gentleman—formed, perhaps, the better part of him. Idleness was an abomination to him; devotion to pleasure, other than the pleasure of money-making, a grievous sin in his eyes. Grindley junior fully intended to do well at Oxford, and might have succeeded. In accusing himself of lack of cleverness, he did himself an injustice. He had brains, he had energy, he had character. Our virtues can be our stumbling-blocks as well as our vices. Young Grindley had one admirable virtue that needs, above all others, careful controlling: he was amiability itself. Before the charm and sweetness of it, Oxford snobbishness went down. The Sauce, against the earnest counsel of its own advertisement, was forgotten; the pickles passed by. To escape the natural result of his popularity would have needed a stronger will than young Grindley possessed. For a time the true state of affairs was hidden from the eye of Grindley senior. To "slack" it this term, with the full determination of "swotting" it the next, is always easy; the difficulty beginning only with the new term. Possibly with luck young Grindley might have retrieved his position and covered up the traces of his folly, but for an unfortunate accident. Returning to college with some other choice spirits at two o'clock in the morning, it occurred to young Grindley that trouble might be saved all round by cutting out a pane of glass with a diamond ring and entering his rooms, which were on the ground-floor, by the window. That, in mistake for his own, he should have selected the bedroom of the College Rector was a misfortune that might have occurred to anyone who had commenced the evening on champagne and finished it on whisky. Young Grindley, having been warned already twice before, was "sent down." And then, of course, the whole history of the three wasted years came out. Old Grindley in his study chair having talked for half an hour at the top of his voice, chose, partly by reason of physical necessity, partly by reason of dormant dramatic instinct, to speak quietly and slowly.

"I'll give you one chance more, my boy, and one only. I've tried you as a gentleman—perhaps that was my mistake. Now I'll try you as a grocer."

"As a what?"

"As a grocer, sir—g-r-o-c-e-r—grocer, a man who stands behind a counter in a white apron and his shirt-sleeves; who sells tea and sugar and candied peel and such-like things to customers—old ladies, little girls; who rises at six in the morning, takes down the shutters, sweeps out the shop, cleans the windows; who has half an hour for his dinner of corned beef and bread; who puts up the shutters at ten o'clock at night, tidies up the shop, has his supper, and goes to bed, feeling his day has not been wasted. I meant to spare you. I was wrong. You shall go through the mill as I went through it. If at the end of two years you've done well with your time, learned something—learned to be a man, at all events—you can come to me and thank me."

"I'm afraid, sir," suggested Grindley junior, whose handsome face during the last few minutes had grown very white, "I might not make a very satisfactory grocer. You see, sir, I've had no experience."

"I am glad you have some sense," returned his father drily. "You are quite right. Even a grocer's business requires learning. It will cost me a little money; but it will be the last I shall ever spend upon you. For the first year you will have to be apprenticed, and I shall allow you something to live on. It shall be more than I had at your age—we'll say a pound a week. After that I shall expect you to keep yourself."

Grindley senior rose. "You need not give me your answer till the evening. You are of age. I have no control over you unless you are willing to agree. You can go my way, or you can go your own."

Young Grindley, who had inherited a good deal of his father's grit, felt very much inclined to go his own; but, hampered on the other hand by the sweetness of disposition he had inherited from his mother, was unable to withstand the argument of that lady's tears, so that evening accepted old Grindley's terms, asking only as a favour that the scene of his probation might be in some out-of-the-way neighbourhood where there would be little chance of his being met by old friends.

"I have thought of all that," answered his father. "My object isn't to humiliate you more than is necessary for your good. The shop I have already selected, on the assumption that you would submit, is as quiet and out-of-the-way as you could wish. It is in a turning off Fetter Lane, where you'll see few other people than printers and caretakers. You'll lodge with a woman, a Mrs. Postwhistle, who seems a very sensible person. She'll board you and lodge you, and every Saturday you'll receive a post-office order for six shillings, out of which you'll find yourself in clothes. You can take with you sufficient to last you for the first six months, but no more. At the end of the year you can change if you like and go to another shop, or make your own arrangements with Mrs. Postwhistle. If all is settled, you go there to-morrow. You go out of this house to-morrow in any event."

Mrs. Postwhistle was a large, placid lady of philosophic temperament. Hitherto the little grocer's shop in Rolls Court, Fetter Lane, had been easy of management by her own unaided efforts; but the neighbourhood was rapidly changing. Other grocers' shops were disappearing one by one, making way for huge blocks of buildings, where hundreds of iron presses, singing day and night, spread to the earth the song of the Mighty Pen. There were hours when the little shop could hardly accommodate its crowd of customers. Mrs. Postwhistle, of a bulk not to be moved quickly, had, after mature consideration, conquering a natural disinclination to change, decided to seek assistance.

Young Grindley, alighting from a four-wheeled cab in Fetter Lane, marched up the court, followed by a weak-kneed wastrel staggering under the weight of a small box. In the doorway of the little shop, young Grindley paused and raised his hat.

"Mrs. Postwhistle?"

The lady, from her chair behind the counter, rose slowly.

"I am Mr. Nathaniel Grindley, the new assistant."

The weak-kneed wastrel let fall the box with a thud upon the floor. Mrs. Postwhistle looked her new assistant up and down.

"Oh!" said Mrs. Postwhistle. "Well, I shouldn't 'ave felt instinctively it must be you, not if I'd 'ad to pick you out of a crowd. But if you tell me so, why, I suppose you are. Come in."

The weak-kneed wastrel, receiving to his astonishment a shilling, departed.

Grindley senior had selected wisely. Mrs. Postwhistle's theory was that although very few people in this world understood their own business, they understood it better than anyone else could understand it for them. If handsome, well-educated young gentlemen, who gave shillings to wastrels, felt they wanted to become smart and capable grocers' assistants, that was their affair. Her business was to teach them their work, and, for her own sake, to see that they did it. A month went by. Mrs. Postwhistle found her new assistant hard-working, willing, somewhat clumsy, but with a smile and a laugh that transformed mistakes, for which another would have been soundly rated, into welcome variations of the day's monotony.

"If you were the sort of woman that cared to make your fortune," said one William Clodd, an old friend of Mrs. Postwhistle's, young Grindley having descended into the cellar to grind coffee, "I'd tell you what to do. Take a bun-shop somewhere in the neighbourhood of a girls' school, and put that assistant of yours in the window. You'd do a roaring business."

"There's a mystery about 'im," said Mrs. Postwhistle.

"Know what it is?"

"If I knew what it was, I shouldn't be calling it a mystery," replied Mrs. Postwhistle, who was a stylist in her way.

"How did you get him? Win him in a raffle?"

"Jones, the agent, sent 'im to me all in a 'urry. An assistant is what I really wanted, not an apprentice; but the premium was good, and the references everything one could desire."

"Grindley, Grindley," murmured Clodd. "Any relation to the Sauce, I wonder?"

"A bit more wholesome, I should say, from the look of him," thought Mrs. Postwhistle.

The question of a post office to meet its growing need had long been under discussion by the neighbourhood. Mrs. Postwhistle was approached upon the subject. Grindley junior, eager for anything that might bring variety into his new, cramped existence, undertook to qualify himself.

Within two months the arrangements were complete. Grindley junior divided his time between dispensing groceries and despatching telegrams and letters, and was grateful for the change.

Grindley junior's mind was fixed upon the fashioning of a cornucopia to receive a quarter of a pound of moist. The customer, an extremely young lady, was seeking to hasten his operations by tapping incessantly with a penny on the counter. It did not hurry him; it only worried him. Grindley junior had not acquired facility in the fashioning of cornucopias—the vertex would invariably become unrolled at the last moment, allowing the contents to dribble out on to the floor or counter. Grindley junior was sweet-tempered as a rule, but when engaged upon the fashioning of a cornucopia, was irritable.

"Hurry up, old man!" urged the extremely young lady. "I've got another appointment in less than half an hour."

"Oh, damn the thing!" said Grindley junior, as the paper for the fourth time reverted to its original shape.

An older lady, standing behind the extremely young lady and holding a telegram-form in her hand, looked indignant.

"Temper, temper," remarked the extremely young lady in reproving tone.

The fifth time was more successful. The extremely young lady went out, commenting upon the waste of time always resulting when boys were employed to do the work of men. The older lady, a haughty person, handed across her telegram with the request that it should be sent off at once.

Grindley junior took his pencil from his pocket and commenced to count.

"*Digniori*, not *digniorus*," commented Grindley junior, correcting the word, "*datur digniori*, dative singular." Grindley junior, still irritable from the struggle with the cornucopia, spoke sharply.

The haughty lady withdrew her eyes from a spot some ten miles beyond the back of the shop, where hitherto they had been resting, and fixed them for the first time upon Grindley junior.

"Thank you," said the haughty lady.

Grindley junior looked up and immediately, to his annoyance, felt that he was blushing. Grindley junior blushed easily—it annoyed him very much.

The haughty young lady also blushed. She did not often blush; when she did, she felt angry with herself.

"A shilling and a penny," demanded Grindley junior.

The haughty young lady counted out the money and departed. Grindley junior, peeping from behind a tin of Abernethy biscuits, noticed that as she passed the window she turned and looked back. She was a very pretty, haughty lady. Grindley junior rather admired dark, level brows and finely cut, tremulous lips, especially when combined with a mass of soft, brown hair, and a rich olive complexion that flushed and paled as one looked at it.

"Might send that telegram off if you've nothing else to do, and there's no particular reason for keeping it back," suggested Mrs. Postwhistle.

"It's only just been handed in," explained Grindley junior, somewhat hurt.

"You've been looking at it for the last five minutes by the clock," said Mrs. Postwhistle.

Grindley junior sat down to the machine. The name and address of the sender was Helvetia Appleyard, Nevill's Court.

Three days passed—singularly empty days they appeared to Grindley junior. On the fourth, Helvetia Appleyard had occasion to despatch another telegram—this time entirely in English.

"One-and-fourpence," sighed Grindley junior.

Miss Appleyard drew forth her purse. The shop was empty.

"How did you come to know Latin?" inquired Miss Appleyard in quite a casual tone.

"I picked up a little at school. It was a phrase I happened to remember," confessed Grindley junior, wondering why he should be feeling ashamed of himself.

"I am always sorry," said Miss Appleyard, "when I see anyone content with the lower life whose talents might, perhaps, fit him for the higher." Something about the tone and manner of Miss Appleyard reminded Grindley junior of his former Rector. Each seemed to have arrived by different roads at the same philosophical aloofness from the world, tempered by chastened interest in human phenomena. "Would you like to try to raise yourself—to improve yourself—to educate yourself?"

An unseen little rogue, who was enjoying himself immensely, whispered to Grindley junior to say nothing but "Yes," he should.

"Will you let me help you?" asked Miss Appleyard. And the simple and heartfelt gratitude with which Grindley junior closed upon the offer proved to Miss Appleyard how true it is that to do good to others is the highest joy.

Miss Appleyard had come prepared for possible acceptance. "You had better begin with this," thought Miss Appleyard. "I have marked the passages that you should learn by heart. Make a note of anything you do not understand, and I will explain it to you when— when next I happen to be passing."

Grindley junior took the book—*Bell's Introduction to the Study of the Classics, for Use of Beginners*—and held it between both hands. Its price was ninepence, but Grindley junior appeared to regard it as a volume of great value.

"It will be hard work at first," Miss Appleyard warned him; "but you must persevere. I have taken an interest in you; you must try not to disappoint me."

And Miss Appleyard, feeling all the sensations of a Hypatia, departed, taking light with her and forgetting to pay for the telegram. Miss Appleyard belonged to the class that young ladies who pride themselves on being tiresomely ignorant and foolish sneer at as "blue-stockings"; that is to say, possessing brains, she had felt the necessity of using them. Solomon Appleyard, widower, a sensible old gentleman, prospering in the printing business, and seeing no necessity for a woman regarding herself as nothing but a doll, a somewhat uninteresting plaything the newness once worn off, thankfully encouraged her. Miss Appleyard had returned from Girton wise in many things, but not in knowledge of the world, which knowledge, too early acquired, does not always make for good in young man or woman. A serious little virgin, Miss Appleyard's ambition was to help the human race. What more useful work could have come to her hand than the raising of this poor but intelligent young grocer's assistant unto the knowledge and the love of higher things. That Grindley junior happened to be an exceedingly good-looking and charming young grocer's assistant had nothing to do with the matter, so Miss Appleyard would have informed you. In her own reasoning she was convinced that her interest in him would have been the same had he been the least attractive of his sex. That there could be danger in such relationship never occurred to her.

Miss Appleyard, a convinced Radical, could not conceive the possibility of a grocer's assistant regarding the daughter of a well-to-do printer in any other light than that of a graciously condescending patron. That there could be danger to herself! you would have been sorry you had suggested the idea. The expression of lofty scorn would have made you feel yourself contemptible.

Miss Appleyard's judgment of mankind was justified; no more promising pupil could have been selected. It was really marvellous the progress made by Grindley junior, under the tutelage of Helvetia Appleyard. His earnestness, his enthusiasm, it quite touched the heart of Helvetia Appleyard. There were many points, it is true, that puzzled Grindley junior. Each time the list of them grew longer. But when Helvetia Appleyard explained them, all became clear. She marvelled herself at her own wisdom, that in a moment made darkness luminous to this young man; his rapt attention while she talked, it was most encouraging. The boy must surely be a genius. To think that but for her intuition he might have remained wasted in a grocer's shop! To rescue such a gem from oblivion, to polish it, was surely the duty of a conscientious Hypatia. Two visits—three visits a week to the little shop in Rolls Court were quite inadequate, so many passages there were requiring elucidation. London in early morning became their classroom: the great, wide, empty, silent streets; the mist-curtained parks, the silence broken only by the blackbirds' amorous whistle, the thrushes' invitation to delight; the old gardens, hidden behind narrow ways. Nathaniel George and Janet Helvetia would rest upon a seat, no living creature within sight, save perhaps a passing policeman or some dissipated cat. Janet Helvetia would expound. Nathaniel George, his fine eyes fixed on hers, seemed never to tire of drinking in her wisdom.

There were times when Janet Helvetia, to reassure herself as to the maidenly correctness of her behaviour, had to recall quite forcibly the fact that she was the daughter of Solomon Appleyard, owner of the big printing establishment; and he a simple grocer. One day, raised a little in the social scale, thanks to her, Nathaniel George would marry someone in his own rank of life. Reflecting upon the future of Nathaniel George, Janet Helvetia could not escape a shade of sadness. It was difficult to imagine precisely the wife she would have chosen for Nathaniel George. She hoped he would do nothing foolish. Rising young men so often marry wives that hamper rather than help them.

One Sunday morning in late autumn, they walked and talked in the shady garden of Lincoln's Inn. Greek they thought it was they had been talking; as a matter of fact, a much older language. A young gardener was watering flowers, and as they passed him he grinned. It was not an offensive grin, rather a sympathetic grin; but Miss Appleyard didn't like being grinned at. What was there to grin at? Her personal appearance? some *gaucherie* in her dress? Impossible. No lady in all St. Dunstan was ever more precise. She glanced at her companion: a clean-looking, well-groomed, well-dressed youth. Suddenly it occurred to Miss Appleyard that she and Grindley junior were holding each other's hand. Miss Appleyard was justly indignant.

"How dare you!" said Miss Appleyard. "I am exceedingly angry with you. How dare you!"

The olive skin was scarlet. There were tears in the hazel eyes.

"Leave me this minute!" commanded Miss Appleyard.

Instead of which, Grindley junior seized both her hands.

"I love you! I adore you! I worship you!" poured forth young Grindley, forgetful of all Miss Appleyard had ever told him concerning the folly of tautology.

"You had no right," said Miss Appleyard.

"I couldn't help it," pleaded young Grindley. "And that isn't the worst."

Miss Appleyard paled visibly. For a grocer's assistant to dare to fall in love with her, especially after all the trouble she had taken with him! What could be worse?

"I'm not a grocer," continued young Grindley, deeply conscious of crime. "I mean, not a real grocer."

And Grindley junior then and there made a clean breast of the whole sad, terrible tale of shameless deceit, practised by the greatest villain the world had ever produced, upon the noblest and most beautiful maiden that ever turned grim London town into a fairy city of enchanted ways.

Not at first could Miss Appleyard entirely grasp it; not till hours later, when she sat alone in her own room, where, fortunately for himself, Grindley junior was not, did the whole force and meaning of the thing come home to her. It was a large room, taking up half of the top story of the big Georgian house in Nevill's Court; but even as it was, Miss Appleyard felt cramped.

"For a year—for nearly a whole year," said Miss Appleyard, addressing the bust of William Shakespeare, "have I been slaving my life out, teaching him elementary Latin and the first five books of Euclid!"

As it has been remarked, it was fortunate for Grindley junior he was out of reach. The bust of William Shakespeare maintained its irritating aspect of benign philosophy.

"I suppose I should," mused Miss Appleyard, "if he had told me at first—as he ought to have told me—of course I should naturally have had nothing more to do with him. I suppose," mused Miss Appleyard, "a man in love, if he is really in love, doesn't quite know what he's doing. I suppose one ought to make allowances. But, oh! when I think of it—"

And then Grindley junior's guardian angel must surely have slipped into the room, for Miss Appleyard, irritated beyond endurance at the philosophical indifference of the bust of William Shakespeare, turned away from it, and as she did so, caught sight of herself in the looking-glass. Miss Appleyard approached the glass a little nearer. A woman's hair is never quite as it should be. Miss Appleyard, standing before the glass, began, she knew not why, to find reasons excusing Grindley junior. After all, was not forgiveness an excellent thing in woman? None of us are quite perfect. The guardian angel of Grindley junior seized the opportunity.

That evening Solomon Appleyard sat upright in his chair, feeling confused. So far as he could understand it, a certain young man, a grocer's assistant, but not a grocer's assistant—but that, of course, was not his fault, his father being an old brute—had behaved most abominably; but not, on reflection, as badly as he might have done, and had acted on the whole very honourably, taking into consideration the fact that one supposed he could hardly help it. Helvetia was, of course, very indignant with him, but on the other hand, did not quite see what else she could have done, she being not at all sure whether she really cared for him or whether she didn't; that everything had been quite proper and would not have happened if she had known it; that everything was her fault, except most things, which weren't; but that of the two she blamed herself entirely, seeing that she could not have guessed anything of the kind. And did he, Solomon Appleyard, think that she ought to be very angry and never marry anybody else, or was she justified in overlooking it and engaging herself to the only man she felt she could ever love?

"You mustn't think, Dad, that I meant to deceive you. I should have told you at the beginning—you know I would—if it hadn't all happened so suddenly."

"Let me see," said Solomon Appleyard, "did you tell me his name, or didn't you?"

"Nathaniel," said Miss Appleyard. "Didn't I mention it?"

"Don't happen to know his surname, do you," inquired her father.

"Grindley," explained Miss Appleyard—"the son of Grindley, the Sauce man."

Miss Appleyard experienced one of the surprises of her life. Never before to her recollection had her father thwarted a single wish of her life. A widower for the last twelve years, his chief delight had been to humour her. His voice, as he passionately swore that never with his consent should his daughter marry the son of Hezekiah Grindley, sounded strange to her. Pleadings, even tears, for the first time in her life proved fruitless.

Here was a pretty kettle of fish! That Grindley junior should defy his own parent, risk possibly the loss of his inheritance, had seemed to both a not improper proceeding. When Nathaniel George had said with fine enthusiasm: "Let him keep his money if he will; I'll make my own way; there isn't enough money in the world to pay for losing you!" Janet Helvetia, though she had expressed disapproval of such unfilial attitude, had in secret sympathised. But for her to disregard the wishes of her own doting father was not to be thought of. What was to be done?

Perhaps one Peter Hope, residing in Gough Square hard by, might help young folks in sore dilemma with wise counsel. Peter Hope, editor and part proprietor of *Good Humour*, one penny weekly, was much esteemed by Solomon Appleyard, printer and publisher of aforesaid paper.

"A good fellow, old Hope," Solomon would often impress upon his managing clerk. "Don't worry him more than you can help; things will improve. We can trust him."

Peter Hope sat at his desk, facing Miss Appleyard. Grindley junior sat on the cushioned seat beneath the middle window. *Good Humour's* sub-editor stood before the fire, her hands behind her back.

The case appeared to Peter Hope to be one of exceeding difficulty.

"Of course," explained Miss Appleyard, "I shall never marry without my father's consent."

Peter Hope thought the resolution most proper.

"On the other hand," continued Miss Appleyard, "nothing shall induce me to marry a man I do not love." Miss Appleyard thought the probabilities were that she would end by becoming a female missionary.

Peter Hope's experience had led him to the conclusion that young people sometimes changed their mind.

The opinion of the House, clearly though silently expressed, was that Peter Hope's experience, as regarded this particular case, counted for nothing.

"I shall go straight to the Governor," explained Grindley junior, "and tell him that I consider myself engaged for life to Miss Appleyard. I know what will happen—I know the sort of idea he has got into his head. He will disown me, and I shall go off to Africa."

Peter Hope was unable to see how Grindley junior's disappearance into the wilds of Africa was going to assist the matter under discussion.

Grindley junior's view was that the wilds of Africa would afford a fitting background to the passing away of a blighted existence.

Peter Hope had a suspicion that Grindley junior had for the moment parted company with that sweet reasonableness that otherwise, so Peter Hope felt sure, was Grindley junior's guiding star.

"I mean it, sir," reasserted Grindley junior. "I am—" Grindley junior was about to add "well educated"; but divining that education was a topic not pleasing at the moment to the ears of Helvetia Appleyard, had tact enough to substitute "not a fool. I can earn my own living; and I should like to get away."

"It seems to me—" said the sub-editor.

"Now, Tommy—I mean Jane," warned her Peter Hope. He always called her Jane in company, unless he was excited. "I know what you are going to say. I won't have it."

"I was only going to say—" urged the sub-editor in tone of one suffering injustice.

"I quite know what you were going to say," retorted Peter hotly. "I can see it by your chin. You are going to take their part—and suggest their acting undutifully towards their parents."

"I wasn't," returned the sub-editor. "I was only—"

"You were," persisted Peter. "I ought not to have allowed you to be present. I might have known you would interfere."

"—going to say we are in want of some help in the office. You know we are. And that if Mr. Grindley would be content with a small salary—"

"Small salary be hanged!" snarled Peter.

"—there would be no need for his going to Africa."

"And how would that help us?" demanded Peter. "Even if the boy were so—so headstrong, so unfilial as to defy his father, who has worked for him all these years, how would that remove the obstacle of Mr. Appleyard's refusal?"

"Why, don't you see—" explained the sub-editor.

"No, I don't," snapped Peter.

"If, on his declaring to his father that nothing will ever induce him to marry any other woman but Miss Appleyard, his father disowns him, as he thinks it likely—"

"A dead cert!" was Grindley junior's conviction.

"Very well; he is no longer old Grindley's son, and what possible objection can Mr. Appleyard have to him then?"

Peter Hope arose and expounded at length and in suitable language the folly and uselessness of the scheme.

But what chance had ever the wisdom of Age against the enthusiasm of Youth, reaching for its object. Poor Peter, expostulating, was swept into the conspiracy. Grindley junior the next morning stood before his father in the private office in High Holborn.

"I am sorry, sir," said Grindley junior, "if I have proved a disappointment to you."

"Damn your sympathy!" said Grindley senior. "Keep it till you are asked for it."

"I hope we part friends, sir," said Grindley junior, holding out his hand.

"Why do you irate me?" asked Grindley senior. "I have thought of nothing but you these five-and-twenty years."

"I don't, sir," answered Grindley junior. "I can't say I love you. It did not seem to me you—you wanted it. But I like you, sir, and I respect you. And—and I'm sorry to have to hurt you, sir."

"And you are determined to give up all your prospects, all the money, for the sake of this—this girl?"

"It doesn't seem like giving up anything, sir," replied Grindley junior, simply.

"It isn't so much as I thought it was going to be," said the old man, after a pause. "Perhaps it is for the best. I might have been more obstinate if things had been going all right. The Lord has chastened me."

"Isn't the business doing well, Dad?" asked the young man, with sorrow in his voice.

"What's it got to do with you?" snapped his father. "You've cut yourself adrift from it. You leave me now I am going down."

Grindley junior, not knowing what to say, put his arms round the little old man.

And in this way Tommy's brilliant scheme fell through and came to naught. Instead, old Grindley visited once again the big house in Nevill's Court, and remained long closeted with old Solomon in the office on the second floor. It was late in the evening when Solomon opened the door and called upstairs to Janet Helvetia to come down.

"I used to know you long ago," said Hezekiah Grindley, rising. "You were quite a little girl then."

Later, the troublesome Sauce disappeared entirely, cut out by newer flavours. Grindley junior studied the printing business. It almost seemed as if old Appleyard had been waiting but for this. Some six months later they found him dead in his counting-house. Grindley junior became the printer and publisher of *Good Humour*.

STORY THE FOURTH

Miss Ramsbotham Gives Her Services

To regard Miss Ramsbotham as a marriageable quantity would have occurred to few men. Endowed by Nature with every feminine quality calculated to inspire liking, she had, on the other hand, been disinherited of every attribute calculated to excite passion. An ugly woman has for some men an attraction; the proof is ever present to our eyes. Miss Ramsbotham was plain but pleasant looking. Large, healthy in mind and body, capable, self-reliant, and cheerful, blessed with a happy disposition together with a keen sense of humour, there was about her absolutely nothing for tenderness to lay hold of. An ideal wife, she was an impossible sweetheart. Every man was her friend. The suggestion that any man could be her lover she herself would have greeted with a clear, ringing laugh.

Not that she held love in despite; for such folly she was possessed of far too much sound sense. "To have somebody in love with you—somebody strong and good," so she would confess to her few close intimates, a dreamy expression clouding for an instant her broad, sunny face, "why, it must be just lovely!" For Miss Ramsbotham was prone to American phraseology, and had even been at some pains, during a six months' journey through the States (whither she had been commissioned by a conscientious trade journal seeking reliable information concerning the condition of female textile workers) to acquire a slight but decided American accent. It was her one affectation, but assumed, as one might feel certain, for a practical and legitimate object.

"You can have no conception," she would explain, laughing, "what a help I find it. 'I'm 'Muriken' is the 'Civis Romanus sum' of the modern woman's world. It opens every door to us. If I ring the bell and say, 'Oh, if you please, I have come to interview Mr. So-and-So for such-and-such a paper,' the footman looks through me at the opposite side of the street, and tells me to wait in the hall while he inquires if Mr. So-and-So will see me or not. But if I say, 'That's my keerd, young man. You tell your master Miss Ramsbotham is waiting for him in the showroom, and will take it real kind if he'll just bustle himself,' the poor fellow walks backwards till he stumbles against the bottom stair, and my gentleman comes down with profuse apologies for having kept me waiting three minutes and a half.

"'And to be in love with someone," she would continue, "someone great that one could look up to and honour and worship—someone that would fill one's whole life, make it beautiful, make every day worth living, I think that would be better still. To work merely for one's self, to think merely for one's self, it is so much less interesting."

Then, at some such point of the argument, Miss Ramsbotham would jump up from her chair and shake herself indignantly.

"Why, what nonsense I'm talking," she would tell herself, and her listeners. "I make a very fair income, have a host of friends, and enjoy every hour of my life. I should like to have been pretty or handsome, of course; but no one can have all the good things of this world, and I have my brains. At one time, perhaps, yes; but now—no, honestly I would not change myself."

Miss Ramsbotham was sorry that no man had ever fallen in love with her, but that she could understand.

"It is quite clear to me." So she had once unburdened herself to her bosom friend. "Man for the purposes of the race has been given two kinds of love, between which, according to his opportunities and temperament, he is free to choose: he can fall down upon his knees and adore physical beauty (for Nature ignores entirely our mental side), or he can take delight in circling with his protecting arm the weak and helpless. Now, I make no appeal to either instinct. I possess neither the charm nor beauty to attract—"

"Beauty," reminded her the bosom friend, consolingly, "dwells in the beholder's eye."

"My dear," cheerfully replied Miss Ramsbotham, "it would have to be an eye of the range and capacity Sam Weller frankly owned up to not possessing—a patent double-million magnifying, capable of seeing through a deal board and round the corner sort of eye—to detect any beauty in me. And I am much too big and sensible for any man not a fool ever to think of wanting to take care of me.

"I believe," remembered Miss Ramsbotham, "if it does not sound like idle boasting, I might have had a husband, of a kind, if Fate had not compelled me to save his life. I met him one year at Huyst, a small, quiet watering-place on the Dutch coast. He would walk always half a step behind me, regarding me out of the corner of his eye quite approvingly at times. He was a widower—a good little man, devoted to his three charming children. They took an immense fancy to me, and I really think I could have got on with him. I am very adaptable, as you know. But it was not to be. He got out of his depth one morning, and unfortunately there was no one within distance but myself who could swim. I knew what the result would be. You remember Labiche's comedy, *Les Voyage de Monsieur Perrichon*? Of course, every man hates having had his life saved, after it is over; and you can imagine how he must hate having it saved by a woman. But what was I to do? In either case he would be lost to me, whether I let him drown or whether I rescued him. So, as it really made no difference, I rescued him. He was very grateful, and left the next morning.

"It is my destiny. No man has ever fallen in love with me, and no man ever will. I used to worry myself about it when I was younger. As a child I hugged to my bosom for years an observation I had overheard an aunt of mine whisper to my mother one afternoon as they sat knitting and talking, not thinking I was listening. 'You never can tell,' murmured my aunt, keeping her eyes carefully fixed upon her needles; 'children change so. I have known the plainest girls grow up into quite beautiful women. I should not worry about it if I were you—not yet awhile.' My mother was not at all a bad-looking woman, and my father was decidedly handsome; so there seemed no reason why I should not hope. I pictured myself the ugly duckling of Andersen's fairy-tale, and every morning on waking I would run straight to my glass and try to persuade myself that the feathers of the swan were beginning at last to show themselves."

Miss Ramsbotham laughed, a genuine laugh of amusement, for of self-pity not a trace was now remaining to her.

"Later I plucked hope again," continued Miss Ramsbotham her confession, "from the reading of a certain school of fiction more popular twenty years ago than now. In these romances the heroine was never what you would call beautiful, unless in common with the hero you happened to possess exceptional powers of observation. But she was better than that, she was good. I do not regard as time wasted the hours I spent studying this quaint literature. It helped me, I am sure, to form habits that have since been of service to me. I made a point, when any young man visitor happened to be staying with us, of rising exceptionally early in the morning, so that I always appeared at the breakfast-table fresh, cheerful, and carefully dressed, with, when possible, a dew-besprinkled flower in my hair to prove that I had already been out in the garden. The effort, as far as the young man visitor was concerned, was always thrown away; as a general rule, he came down late himself, and generally too drowsy to notice anything much. But it was excellent practice for me. I wake now at seven o'clock as a matter of course, whatever time I go to bed. I made my own dresses and most of our cakes, and took care to let everybody know it. Though I say it who should not, I play and sing rather well. I certainly was never a fool. I had no little brothers and sisters to whom to be exceptionally devoted, but I had my cousins about the house as much as possible, and damaged their characters, if anything, by over-indulgence. My dear, it never caught even a curate! I am not one of those women to run down men; I think them delightful creatures, and in a general way I find them very intelligent. But where their hearts are concerned it is the girl with the frizzy hair, who wants two people to help her over the stile, that is their idea of an angel. No man could fall in love with me; he couldn't if he tried. That I can understand; but"—Miss Ramsbotham sunk her voice to a more confidential tone—"what I cannot understand is that I have never fallen in love with any man, because I like them all."

"You have given the explanation yourself," suggested the bosom friend—one Susan Fossett, the "Aunt Emma" of *The Ladies' Journal*, a nice woman, but talkative. "You are too sensible."

Miss Ramsbotham shook her head, "I should just love to fall in love. When I think about it, I feel quite ashamed of myself for not having done so."

Whether it was this idea, namely, that it was her duty, or whether it was that passion came to her, unsought, somewhat late in life, and therefore all the stronger, she herself would perhaps have been unable to declare. Certain only it is that at over thirty years of age this clever, sensible, clear-seeing woman fell to sighing and blushing, starting and stammering at the sounding of a name, as though for all the world she had been a love-sick girl in her teens.

Susan Fossett, her bosom friend, brought the strange tidings to Bohemia one foggy November afternoon, her opportunity being a tea-party given by Peter Hope to commemorate the birthday of his adopted daughter and sub-editor, Jane Helen, commonly called Tommy. The actual date of Tommy's birthday was known only to the gods; but out of the London mist to wifeless, childless Peter she had come the evening of a certain November the eighteenth, and therefore by Peter and his friends November the eighteenth had been marked upon the calendar as a day on which they should rejoice together.

"It is bound to leak out sooner or later," Susan Fossett was convinced, "so I may as well tell you: that gaby Mary Ramsbotham has got herself engaged."

"Nonsense!" was Peter Hope's involuntary ejaculation.

"Precisely what I mean to tell her the very next time I see her," added Susan.

"Who to?" demanded Tommy.

"You mean 'to whom.' The preeposition governs the objective case," corrected her James Douglas McTear, commonly called "The Wee Laddie," who himself wrote English better than he spoke it.

"I meant 'to whom,'" explained Tommy.

"Ye didna say it," persisted the Wee Laddie.

"I don't know to whom," replied Miss Ramsbotham's bosom friend, sipping tea and breathing indignation. "To something idiotic and incongruous that will make her life a misery to her."

Somerville, the briefless, held that in the absence of all data such conclusion was unjustifiable.

"If it had been to anything sensible," was Miss Fossett's opinion, "she would not have kept me in the dark about it, to spring it upon me like a bombshell. I've never had so much as a hint from her until I received this absurd scrawl an hour ago."

Miss Fossett produced from her bag a letter written in pencil.

"There can be no harm in your hearing it," was Miss Fossett's excuse; "it will give you an idea of the state of the poor thing's mind."

The tea-drinkers left their cups and gathered round her. "Dear Susan," read Miss Fossett, "I shall not be able to be with you to-morrow. Please get me out of it nicely. I can't remember at the moment what it is. You'll be surprised to hear that I'm *engaged*—to be married, I mean, I can hardly *realise* it. I hardly seem to know where I am. Have just made up my mind to run down to Yorkshire and see grandmamma. I must do *something*. I must *talk* to *somebody* and—forgive me, dear—but you *are* so sensible, and just now—well I don't *feel* sensible. Will tell you all about it when I see you—next week, perhaps. You must *try* to like him. He is *so* handsome and *really* clever—in his own way. Don't scold me. I never thought it possible that *anyone* could be so happy. It's quite a different sort of happiness to *any* other sort of happiness. I don't know how to describe it. Please ask Burcot to let me off the antequarian congress. I feel I should do it badly. I am so thankful he has *no* relatives—in England. I should have been so *terribly* nervous. Twelve hours ago I could not have *dreamt* of it, and now I walk on tiptoe for fear of waking up. Did I leave my chinchilla at your rooms? Don't be angry with me. I should have told you if I had known. In haste. Yours, Mary."

"It's dated from Marylebone Road, and yesterday afternoon she did leave her chinchilla in my rooms, which makes me think it really must be from Mary Ramsbotham. Otherwise I should have my doubts," added Miss Fossett, as she folded up the letter and replaced it in her bag.

"Id is love!" was the explanation of Dr. William Smith, his round, red face illuminated with poetic ecstasy. "Love has gone to her—has dransformed her once again into the leedle maid."

"Love," retorted Susan Fossett, "doesn't transform an intelligent, educated woman into a person who writes a letter all in jerks, under-lines every other word, spells antiquarian with an 'e,' and Burcott's name, whom she has known for the last eight years, with only one 't.' The woman has gone stark, staring mad!"

"We must wait until we have seen him," was Peter's judicious view. "I should be so glad to think that the dear lady was happy."

"So should I," added Miss Fossett drily.

"One of the most sensible women I have ever met," commented William Clodd. "Lucky man, whoever he is. Half wish I'd thought of it myself."

"I am not saying that he isn't," retorted Miss Fossett. "It isn't him I'm worrying about."

"I preesume you mean 'he,'" suggested the Wee Laddie. "The verb 'to be'—"

"For goodness' sake," suggested Miss Fossett to Tommy, "give that man something to eat or drink. That's the worst of people who take up grammar late in life. Like all converts, they become fanatical."

"She's a ripping good sort, is Mary Ramsbotham," exclaimed Grindley junior, printer and publisher of *Good Humour*. "The marvel to me is that no man hitherto has had the sense to want her."

"Oh, you men!" cried Miss Fossett. "A pretty face and an empty head is all you want."

"Must they always go together?" laughed Mrs. Grindley junior, *nee* Helvetia Appleyard.

"Exceptions prove the rule," grunted Miss Fossett.

"What a happy saying that is," smiled Mrs. Grindley junior. "I wonder sometimes how conversation was ever carried on before it was invented."

"De man who would fall in love wid our dear frent Mary," thought Dr. Smith, "he must be quite egsceptional."

"You needn't talk about her as if she was a monster—I mean were," corrected herself Miss Fossett, with a hasty glance towards the Wee Laddie. "There isn't a man I know that's worthy of her."

"I mean," explained the doctor, "dat he must be a man of character—of brain. Id is de noble man dat is attracted by de noble woman."

"By the chorus-girl more often," suggested Miss Fossett.

"We must hope for the best," counselled Peter. "I cannot believe that a clever, capable woman like Mary Ramsbotham would make a fool of herself."

"From what I have seen," replied Miss Fossett, "it's just the clever people—as regards this particular matter—who do make fools of themselves."

Unfortunately Miss Fossett's judgment proved to be correct. On being introduced a fortnight later to Miss Ramsbotham's fiancé, the impulse of Bohemia was to exclaim, "Great Scott! Whatever in the name of—" Then on catching sight of Miss Ramsbotham's trans-figured face and trembling hands Bohemia recollected itself in time to murmur instead: "Delighted, I'm sure!" and to offer mechanical congratulations. Reginald Peters was a pretty but remarkably fool-ish-looking lad of about two-and-twenty, with curly hair and reced-ing chin; but to Miss Ramsbotham evidently a promising Apollo. Her first meeting with him had taken place at one of the many po-litical debating societies then in fashion, attendance at which Miss Ramsbotham found useful for purposes of journalistic "copy." Miss Ramsbotham, hitherto a Radical of pronounced views, he had suc-ceeded under three months in converting into a strong supporter of the Gentlemanly Party. His feeble political platitudes, which a little while before she would have seized upon merrily to ridicule, she now sat drinking in, her plain face suffused with admiration. Away from him and in connection with those subjects—somewhat numerous—about which he knew little and cared less, she retained her sense and humour; but in his presence she remained comparatively speechless, gazing up into his somewhat watery eyes with the grateful expres-sion of one learning wisdom from a master.

Her absurd adoration—irritating beyond measure to her friends, and which even to her lover, had he possessed a grain of sense, would have appeared ridiculous—to Master Peters was evidently a gratification. Of selfish, exacting nature, he must have found the services of this brilliant woman of the world of much practical ad-vantage. Knowing all the most interesting people in London, it was her pride and pleasure to introduce him everywhere. Her friends put up with him for her sake; to please her made him welcome, did their best to like him, and disguised their failure. The free entry to a places of amusement saved his limited purse. Her influence, he had instinct enough to perceive, could not fail to be of use to him in his profession: that of a barrister. She praised him to prominent solici-tors, took him to tea with judges' wives, interested examiners on his behalf. In return he overlooked her many disadvantages, and did not fail to let her know it. Miss Ramsbotham's gratitude was boundless.

"I do so wish I were younger and better looking," she sighed to the bosom friend. "For myself, I don't mind; I have got used to it. But it is so hard on Reggie. He feels it, I know he does, though he never openly complains."

"He would be a cad if he did," answered Susan Fossett, who having tried conscientiously for a month to tolerate the fellow, had in the end declared her inability even to do more than avoid open expression of cordial dislike. "Added to which I don't quite see of what use it would be. You never told him you were young and pretty, did you?"

"I told him, my dear," replied Miss Ramsbotham, "the actual truth. I don't want to take any credit for doing so; it seemed the best course. You see, unfortunately, I look my age. With most men it would have made a difference. You have no idea how good he is. He assured me he had engaged himself to me with his eyes open, and that there was no need to dwell upon unpleasant topics. It is so wonderful to me that he should care for me—he who could have half the women in London at his feet."

"Yes, he's the type that would attract them, I daresay," agreed Susan Fossett. "But are you quite sure that he does?—care for you, I mean."

"My dear," returned Miss Ramsbotham, "you remember Rochefoucauld's definition. 'One loves, the other consents to be loved.' If he will only let me do that I shall be content. It is more than I had any right to expect."

"Oh, you are a fool," told her bluntly her bosom friend.

"I know I am," admitted Miss Ramsbotham; "but I had no idea that being a fool was so delightful."

Bohemia grew day by day more indignant and amazed. Young Peters was not even a gentleman. All the little offices of courtship he left to her. It was she who helped him on with his coat, and afterwards adjusted her own cloak; she who carried the parcel, she who followed into and out of the restaurant. Only when he thought anyone was watching would he make any attempt to behave to her with even ordinary courtesy. He bullied her, contradicted her in public, ignored her openly. Bohemia fumed with impotent rage, yet was bound to confess that so far as Miss Ramsbotham herself was concerned he had done more to make her happy than had ever all Bohemia put together. A tender light took up its dwelling in her eyes, which for the first time it was noticed were singularly deep and expressive. The blood, of which she possessed if anything too much, now came and went, so that her cheeks, in place of their insistent red, took on a varied pink and white. Life had entered her thick dark hair, giving to it shade and shadow.

The woman began to grow younger. She put on flesh. Sex, hitherto dormant, began to show itself; femininities peeped out. New tones, suggesting possibilities, crept into her voice. Bohemia congratulated itself that the affair, after all, might turn out well.

Then Master Peters spoiled everything by showing a better side to his nature, and, careless of all worldly considerations, falling in love himself, honestly, with a girl at the bun shop. He did the best thing under the circumstances that he could have done: told Miss Ramsbotham the plain truth, and left the decision in her hands.

Miss Ramsbotham acted as anyone who knew her would have foretold. Possibly, in the silence of her delightful little four-roomed flat over the tailor's shop in Marylebone Road, her sober, worthy maid dismissed for a holiday, she may have shed some tears; but, if so, no trace of them was allowed to mar the peace of mind of Mr. Peters. She merely thanked him for being frank with her, and by a little present pain saving them both a future of disaster. It was quite understandable; she knew he had never really been in love with her. She had thought him the type of man that never does fall in love, as the word is generally understood—Miss Ramsbotham did not add, with anyone except himself—and had that been the case, and he content merely to be loved, they might have been happy together. As it was—well, it was fortunate he had found out the truth before it was too late. Now, would he take her advice?

Mr. Peters was genuinely grateful, as well he might be, and would consent to any suggestion that Miss Ramsbotham might make; felt he had behaved shabbily, was very much ashamed of himself, would be guided in all things by Miss Ramsbotham, whom he should always regard as the truest of friends, and so on.

Miss Ramsbotham's suggestion was this: Mr. Peters, no more robust of body than of mind, had been speaking for some time past of travel. Having nothing to do now but to wait for briefs, why not take this opportunity of visiting his only well-to-do relative, a Canadian farmer. Meanwhile, let Miss Peggy leave the bun shop and take up her residence in Miss Ramsbotham's flat. Let there be no engagement—merely an understanding. The girl was pretty, charming, good, Miss Ramsbotham felt sure; but—well, a little education, a little training in manners and behaviour would not be amiss, would it? If, on returning at the end of six months or a year, Mr. Peters was still of the same mind, and Peggy also wishful, the affair would be easier, would it not?

There followed further expressions of eternal gratitude. Miss Ramsbotham swept all such aside. It would be pleasant to have a bright young girl to live with her; teaching, moulding such an one would be a pleasant occupation.

And thus it came to pass that Mr. Reginald Peters disappeared for a while from Bohemia, to the regret of but few, and there entered into it one Peggy Nutcombe, as pretty a child as ever gladdened the eye of man. She had wavy, flaxen hair, a complexion that might have been manufactured from the essence of wild roses, the nose that Tennyson bestows upon his miller's daughter, and a mouth worthy of the Lowther Arcade in its days of glory. Add to this the quick grace of a kitten, with the appealing helplessness of a baby in its first short frock, and you will be able to forgive Mr. Reginald Peters his faithlessness. Bohemia looked from one to the other—from the fairy to the woman—and ceased to blame. That the fairy was as stupid as a camel, as selfish as a pig, and as lazy as a nigger Bohemia did not know; nor—so long as her figure and complexion remained what it was—would its judgment have been influenced, even if it had. I speak of the Bohemian male.

But that is just what her figure and complexion did not do. Mr. Reginald Peters, finding his uncle old, feeble, and inclined to be fond, deemed it to his advantage to stay longer than he had intended. Twelve months went by. Miss Peggy was losing her kittenish grace, was becoming lumpy. A couple of pimples—one near the right-hand corner of her rosebud mouth, and another on the left-hand side of her tip-tilted nose—marred her baby face. At the end of another six months the men called her plump, and the women fat. Her walk was degenerating into a waddle; stairs caused her to grunt. She took to breathing with her mouth, and Bohemia noticed that her teeth were small, badly coloured, and uneven. The pimples grew in size and number. The cream and white of her complexion was merging into a general yellow. A certain greasiness of skin was manifesting itself. Babyish ways in connection with a woman who must have weighed about eleven stone struck Bohemia as incongruous. Her manners, judged alone, had improved. But they had not improved her. They did not belong to her; they did not fit her. They sat on her as Sunday broadcloth on a yokel. She had learned to employ her "h's" correctly, and to speak good grammar. This gave to her conversation a painfully artificial air. The little learning she had absorbed was sufficient to bestow upon her an angry consciousness of her own invincible ignorance.

Meanwhile, Miss Ramsbotham had continued upon her course of rejuvenation. At twenty-nine she had looked thirty-five; at thirty-two she looked not a day older than five-and-twenty. Bohemia felt that should she retrograde further at the same rate she would soon have to shorten her frocks and let down her hair. A nervous excitability had taken possession of her that was playing strange freaks not only with her body, but with her mind. What it gave to the one it seemed to take from the other. Old friends, accustomed to enjoy with her the luxury of plain speech, wondered in vain what they had done to offend her. Her desire was now towards new friends, new faces. Her sense of humour appeared to be departing from her; it became unsafe to jest with her. On the other hand, she showed herself greedy for admiration and flattery. Her former chums stepped back astonished to watch brainless young fops making their way with her by complimenting her upon her blouse, or whispering to her some trite nonsense about her eyelashes. From her work she took a good percentage of her brain power to bestow it on her clothes. Of course, she was successful. Her dresses suited her, showed her to the best advantage. Beautiful she could never be, and had sense enough to know it; but a charming, distinguished-looking woman she had already become. Also, she was on the high road to becoming a vain, egotistical, commonplace woman.

It was during the process of this, her metamorphosis, that Peter Hope one evening received a note from her announcing her intention of visiting him the next morning at the editorial office of *Good Humour*. She added in a postscript that she would prefer the interview to be private.

Punctually to the time appointed Miss Ramsbotham arrived. Miss Ramsbotham, contrary to her custom, opened conversation with the weather. Miss Ramsbotham was of opinion that there was every possibility of rain. Peter Hope's experience was that there was always possibility of rain.

"How is the Paper doing?" demanded Miss Ramsbotham.

The Paper—for a paper not yet two years old—was doing well. "We expect very shortly—very shortly indeed," explained Peter Hope, "to turn the corner."

"Ah! that 'corner,'" sympathised Miss Ramsbotham.

"I confess," smiled Peter Hope, "it doesn't seem to be exactly a right-angled corner. One reaches it as one thinks. But it takes some getting round—what I should describe as a cornery corner."

"What you want," thought Miss Ramsbotham, "are one or two popular features."

"Popular features," agreed Peter guardedly, scenting temptation, "are not to be despised, provided one steers clear of the vulgar and the commonplace."

"A Ladies' Page!" suggested Miss Ramsbotham—"a page that should make the woman buy it. The women, believe me, are going to be of more and more importance to the weekly press."

"But why should she want a special page to herself?" demanded Peter Hope. "Why should not the paper as a whole appeal to her?"

"It doesn't," was all Miss Ramsbotham could offer in explanation.

"We give her literature and the drama, poetry, fiction, the higher politics, the—"

"I know, I know," interrupted Miss Ramsbotham, who of late, among other failings new to her, had developed a tendency to-wards impatience; "but she gets all that in half a dozen other papers. I have thought it out." Miss Ramsbotham leaned further across the editorial desk and sunk her voice unconsciously to a confidential whisper. "Tell her the coming fashions. Discuss the question whether hat or bonnet makes you look the younger. Tell her whether red hair or black is to be the new colour, what size waist is being worn by the best people. Oh, come!" laughed Miss Ramsbotham in answer to Peter's shocked expression; "one can-not reform the world and human nature all at once. You must appeal to people's folly in order to get them to listen to your wis-dom. Make your paper a success first. You can make it a power afterwards."

"But," argued Peter, "there are already such papers—papers de-voted to—to that sort of thing, and to nothing else."

"At sixpence!" replied the practical Miss Ramsbotham. "I am thinking of the lower middle-class woman who has twenty pounds a year to spend on dress, and who takes twelve hours a day to think about it, poor creature. My dear friend, there is a fortune in it. Think of the advertisements."

Poor Peter groaned—old Peter, the dreamer of dreams. But for thought of Tommy! one day to be left alone to battle with a stony-eyed, deaf world, Peter most assuredly would have risen in his wrath, would have said to his distinguished-looking temptress, "Get thee behind me, Miss Ramsbotham. My journalistic instinct whispers to me that your scheme, judged by the mammon of unrighteousness, is good. It is a new departure. Ten years hence half the London journals will have adopted it. There is money in it. But what of that? Shall I for mere dross sell my editorial soul, turn the temple of the Mighty Pen into a den of—of milliners! Good morning, Miss Ramsbotham. I grieve for you. I grieve for you as for a fellow-worker once inspired by devotion to a noble calling, who has fallen from her high estate. Good morning, madam."

So Peter thought as he sat tattooing with his finger-tips upon the desk; but only said—

"It would have to be well done."

"Everything would depend upon how it was done," agreed Miss Ramsbotham. "Badly done, the idea would be wasted. You would be merely giving it away to some other paper."

"Do you know of anyone?" queried Peter.

"I was thinking of myself," answered Miss Ramsbotham.

"I am sorry," said Peter Hope.

"Why?" demanded Miss Ramsbotham. "Don't you think I could do it?"

"I think," said Peter, "no one could do it better. I am sorry you should wish to do it—that is all."

"I want to do it," replied Miss Ramsbotham, a note of doggedness in her voice.

"How much do you propose to charge me?" Peter smiled.

"Nothing."

"My dear lady—"

"I could not in conscience," explained Miss Ramsbotham, "take payment from both sides. I am going to make a good deal out of it. I am going to make out of it at least three hundred a year, and they will be glad to pay it."

"Who will?"

"The dressmakers. I shall be one of the most stylish women in London," laughed Miss Ramsbotham.

"You used to be a sensible woman," Peter reminded her.

"I want to live."

"Can't you manage to do it without—without being a fool, my dear."

"No," answered Miss Ramsbotham, "a woman can't. I've tried it."

"Very well," agreed Peter, "be it so."

Peter had risen. He laid his shapely, white old hand upon the woman's shoulder. "Tell me when you want to give it up. I shall be glad."

Thus it was arranged. *Good Humour* gained circulation and—of more importance yet—advertisements; and Miss Ramsbotham, as she had predicted, the reputation of being one of the best-dressed women in London. Her reason for desiring such reputation Peter Hope had shrewdly guessed. Two months later his suspicions were confirmed. Mr. Reginald Peters, his uncle being dead, was on his way back to England.

His return was awaited with impatience only by the occupants of the little flat in the Marylebone Road; and between these two the difference of symptom was marked. Mistress Peggy, too stupid to comprehend the change that had been taking place in her, looked forward to her lover's arrival with delight. Mr. Reginald Peters, independently of his profession, was in consequence of his uncle's death a man of means. Miss Ramsbotham's tutelage, which had always been distasteful to her, would now be at an end. She would be a "lady" in the true sense of the word—according to Miss Peggy's definition, a woman with nothing to do but eat and drink, and nothing to think of but dress. Miss Ramsbotham, on the other hand, who might have anticipated the home-coming of her quondam admirer with hope, exhibited a strange condition of alarmed misery, which increased from day to day as the date drew nearer.

The meeting—whether by design or accident was never known—took place at an evening party given by the proprietors of a new journal. The circumstance was certainly unfortunate for poor Peggy, whom Bohemia began to pity. Mr. Peters, knowing both women would be there and so on the look-out, saw in the distance among the crowd of notabilities a superbly millinered, tall, graceful woman, whose face recalled sensations he could not for the moment place. Chiefly noticeable about her were her exquisite neck and arms, and the air of perfect breeding with which she moved, talking and laughing, through the distinguished, fashionable throng. Beside her strutted, nervously aggressive, a vulgar, fat, pimply, shapeless young woman, attracting universal attention by the incongruity of her presence in the room. On being greeted by the graceful lady of the neck and arms, the conviction forced itself upon him that this could be no other than the once Miss Ramsbotham, plain of face and indifferent of dress, whose very appearance he had almost forgotten. On being greeted gushingly as "Reggie" by the sallow-complexioned, over-dressed young woman he bowed with evident astonishment, and apologised for a memory that, so he assured the lady, had always been to him a source of despair.

Of course, he thanked his stars—and Miss Ramsbotham—that the engagement had never been formal. So far as Mr. Peters was concerned, there was an end to Mistress Peggy's dream of an existence of everlasting breakfasts in bed. Leaving the Ramsbotham flat, she returned to the maternal roof, and there a course of hard work and plain living tended greatly to improve her figure and complexion; so that in course of time, the gods smiling again upon her, she married a foreman printer, and passes out of this story.

Meanwhile, Mr. Reginald Peters—older, and the possessor, perhaps, of more sense—looked at Miss Ramsbotham with new eyes, and now not tolerated but desired her. Bohemia waited to assist at the happy termination of a pretty and somewhat novel romance. Miss Ramsbotham had shown no sign of being attracted elsewhere. Flattery, compliment, she continued to welcome; but merely, so it seemed, as favourable criticism. Suitors more fit and proper were now not lacking, for Miss Ramsbotham, though a woman less desirable when won, came readily to the thought of wooing. But to all such she turned a laughing face.

"I like her for it," declared Susan Fossett; "and he has improved—there was room for it—though I wish it could have been some other. There was Jack Herring—it would have been so much more suitable. Or even Joe, in spite of his size. But it's her wedding, not ours; and she will never care for anyone else."

And Bohemia bought its presents, and had them ready, but never gave them. A few months later Mr. Reginald Peters returned to Canada, a bachelor. Miss Ramsbotham expressed her desire for another private interview with Peter Hope.

"I may as well keep on the Letter to Clorinda," thought Miss Ramsbotham. "I have got into the knack of it. But I will get you to pay me for it in the ordinary way."

"I would rather have done so from the beginning," explained Peter.

"I know. I could not in conscience, as I told you, take from both sides. For the future—well, they have said nothing; but I expect they are beginning to get tired of it."

"And you!" questioned Peter.

"Yes. I am tired of it myself," laughed Miss Ramsbotham. "Life isn't long enough to be a well-dressed woman."

"You have done with all that?"

"I hope so," answered Miss Ramsbotham.

"And don't want to talk any more about it?" suggested Peter.

"Not just at present. I should find it so difficult to explain."

By others, less sympathetic than old Peter, vigorous attempts were made to solve the mystery. Miss Ramsbotham took enjoyment in cleverly evading these tormentors. Thwarted at every point, the gossips turned to other themes. Miss Ramsbotham found interest once again in the higher branches of her calling; became again, by slow degrees, the sensible, frank, 'good sort' that Bohemia had known, liked, respected—everything but loved.

Years later, to Susan Fossett, the case was made clear; and through Susan Fossett, a nice enough woman but talkative, those few still interested learned the explanation.

"Love," said Miss Ramsbotham to the bosom friend, "is not regulated by reason. As you say, there were many men I might have married with much more hope of happiness. But I never cared for any other man. He was not intellectual, was egotistical, possibly enough selfish. The man should always be older than the woman; he was younger, and he was a weak character. Yet I loved him."

"I am glad you didn't marry him," said the bosom friend.

"So am I," agreed Miss Ramsbotham.

"If you can't trust me," had said the bosom friend at this point, "don't."

"I meant to do right," said Miss Ramsbotham, "upon my word of honour I did, in the beginning."

"I don't understand," said the bosom friend.

"If she had been my own child," continued Miss Ramsbotham, "I could not have done more—in the beginning. I tried to teach her, to put some sense into her. Lord! the hours I wasted on that little idiot! I marvel at my own patience. She was nothing but an animal. An animal! she had only an animal's vices. To eat and drink and sleep was her idea of happiness; her one ambition male admiration, and she hadn't character enough to put sufficient curb upon her stomach to retain it. I reasoned with her, I pleaded with her, I bullied her. Had I persisted I might have succeeded by sheer physical and mental strength in restraining her from ruining herself. I was winning. I had made her frightened of me. Had I gone on, I might have won. By dragging her out of bed in the morning, by insisting upon her taking exercise, by regulating every particle of food and drink she put into her mouth, I kept the little beast in good condition for nearly three months. Then, I had to go away into the country for a few days; she swore she would obey my instructions. When I came back I found she had been in bed most of the time, and had been living chiefly on chocolate and cakes. She was curled up asleep in an easy-chair, snoring with her mouth wide open, when I opened the door. And at sight of that picture the devil came to me and tempted me. Why should I waste my time, wear myself out in mind and body, that the man I loved should marry a pig because it looked like an angel? 'Six months' wallowing according to its own desires would reveal it in its true shape. So from that day I left it to itself. No, worse than that—I don't want to spare myself—I encouraged her. I let her have a fire in her bedroom, and half her meals in bed. I let her have chocolate with tablespoonfuls of cream floating on the top: she loved it. She was never really happy except when eating. I let her order her own meals. I took a fiendish delight watching the dainty limbs turning to shapeless fat, the pink-and-white complexion growing blotchy. It is flesh that man loves; brain and mind and heart and soul! he never thinks of them. This little pink-and-white sow could have cut me out with Solomon himself. Why should such creatures have the world arranged for them, and we not be allowed to use our brains in our own defence? But for my looking-glass I might have resisted the temptation, but I always had something of the man in me: the sport of the thing appealed to me. I suppose it was the nervous excitement under which I was living that was changing me. All my sap was going into my body. Given sufficient time, I might meet her with her own weapons, animal against animal. Well, you know the result: I won. There was no doubt about his being in love with me. His eyes would follow me round the room, feasting on me. I had become a fine animal. Men desired me, Do you know why I refused him? He was in every way a better man than the silly boy I had fallen in love with; but he came back with a couple of false teeth: I saw the gold setting one day when he opened his mouth to laugh. I don't say for a moment, my dear, there is no such thing as love—love pure, ennobling, worthy of men and women, its roots in the heart and nowhere else. But that love I had missed; and the other! I saw it in its true light. I had fallen in love with him because he was a pretty, curly-headed boy. He had fallen in love with Peggy when she was pink-and-white and slim. I shall always see the look that came into his eyes when she spoke to him at the hotel, the look of disgust and loathing. The girl was the same; it was only her body that had grown older. I could see his eyes fixed upon my arms and neck. I had got to grow old in time, brown skinned, and wrinkled. I thought of him, growing bald, fat—"

"If you had fallen in love with the right man," had said Susan Fossett, "those ideas would not have come to you."

"I know," said Miss Ramsbotham. "He will have to like me thin and in these clothes, just because I am nice, and good company, and helpful. That is the man I am waiting for."

He never came along. A charming, bright-eyed, white-haired lady occupies alone a little flat in the Marylebone Road, looks in occasionally at the Writers' Club. She is still Miss Ramsbotham.

Bald-headed gentlemen feel young again talking to her: she is so sympathetic, so big-minded, so understanding. Then, hearing the clock strike, tear themselves from her with a sigh, and return home—some of them—to stupid shrewish wives.

STORY THE FIFTH

Joey Loveredge Agrees— on Certain Terms—to Join the Company

THE MOST POPULAR MEMBER of the Autolycus Club was undoubtedly Joseph Loveredge. Small, chubby, clean-shaven, his somewhat longish, soft, brown hair parted in the middle, strangers fell into the error of assuming him to be younger than he really was. It is on record that a leading lady novelist—accepting her at her own estimate—irritated by his polite but firm refusal to allow her entrance into his own editorial office without appointment, had once boxed his ears, under the impression that he was his own office-boy. Guests to the Autolycus Club, on being introduced to him, would give to him kind messages to take home to his father, with whom they remembered having been at school together. This sort of thing might have annoyed anyone with less sense of humour. Joseph Loveredge would tell such stories himself, keenly enjoying the jest—was even suspected of inventing some of the more improbable. Another fact tending to the popularity of Joseph Loveredge among all classes, over and above his amiability, his wit, his genuine kindliness, and his never-failing fund of good stories, was that by care and inclination he had succeeded in remaining a bachelor. Many had been the attempts to capture him; nor with the passing of the years had interest in the sport shown any sign of diminution. Well over the frailties and distempers so dangerous to youth, of staid and sober habits, with an ever-increasing capital invested in sound securities, together with an ever-increasing income from his pen, with a tastefully furnished house overlooking Regent's Park, an excellent and devoted cook and house-keeper, and relatives mostly settled in the Colonies, Joseph Loveredge, though inexperienced girls might pass him by with a contemptuous sniff, was recognised by ladies of maturer judgment as a prize not too often dangled before the eyes of spinsterhood. Old foxes—so we are assured by kind-hearted country gentlemen—rather enjoy than otherwise a day with the hounds. However that may be, certain it is that Joseph Loveredge, confident of himself, one presumes, showed no particular disinclination to the chase. Perhaps on the whole he preferred the society of his own sex, with whom he could laugh and jest with more freedom, to whom he could tell his stories as they came to him without the trouble of having to turn them over first in his own mind; but, on the other hand, Joey made no attempt to avoid female company whenever it came his way; and then no cavalier could render himself more agreeable, more unobtrusively attentive. Younger men stood by, in envious admiration of the ease with which in five minutes he would establish himself on terms of cosy friendship with the brilliant beauty before whose gracious coldness they had stood shivering for months; the daring with which he would tuck under his arm, so to speak, the prettiest girl in the room, smooth down as if by magic her hundred prickles, and tease her out of her overwhelming sense of her own self-importance. The secret of his success was, probably, that he was not afraid of them. Desiring nothing from them beyond companionableness, a reasonable amount of appreciation for his jokes—which without being exceptionally stupid they would have found it difficult to withhold—with just sufficient information and intelligence to make conversation interesting, there was nothing about him by which they could lay hold of him. Of course, that rendered them particularly anxious to lay hold of him. Joseph's lady friends might, roughly speaking, be divided into two groups: the unmarried, who wanted to marry him to themselves; and the married, who wanted to marry him to somebody else. It would be a social disaster, the latter had agreed among themselves, if Joseph Loveredge should never wed.

"He would make such an excellent husband for poor Bridget."

"Or Gladys. I wonder how old Gladys really is?"

"Such a nice, kind little man."

"And when one thinks of the sort of men that *are* married, it does seem such a pity!"

"I wonder why he never has married, because he's just the sort of man you'd think *would* have married."

"I wonder if he ever was in love."

"Oh, my dear, you don't mean to tell me that a man has reached the age of forty without ever being in love!"

The ladies would sigh.

"I do hope if ever he does marry, it will be somebody nice. Men are so easily deceived."

"I shouldn't be surprised myself a bit if something came of it with Bridget. She's a dear girl, Bridget—so genuine."

"Well, I think myself, dear, if it's anyone, it's Gladys. I should be so glad to see poor dear Gladys settled."

The unmarried kept their thoughts more to themselves. Each one, upon reflection, saw ground for thinking that Joseph Loveredge had given proof of feeling preference for herself. The irritating thing was that, on further reflection, it was equally clear that Joseph Loveredge had shown signs of preferring most of the others.

Meanwhile Joseph Loveredge went undisturbed upon his way. At eight o'clock in the morning Joseph's housekeeper entered the room with a cup of tea and a dry biscuit. At eight-fifteen Joseph Loveredge arose and performed complicated exercises on an india-rubber pulley, warranted, if persevered in, to bestow grace upon the figure and elasticity upon the limbs. Joseph Loveredge persevered steadily, and had done so for years, and was himself contented with the result, which, seeing it concerned nobody else, was all that could be desired. At half-past eight on Mondays, Wednesdays, and Fridays, Joseph Loveredge breakfasted on one cup of tea, brewed by himself; one egg, boiled by himself; and two pieces of toast, the first one spread with marmalade, the second with butter. On Tuesdays, Thursdays, and Saturdays Joseph Loveredge discarded eggs and ate a rasher of bacon. On Sundays Joseph Loveredge had both eggs and bacon, but then allowed himself half an hour longer for reading the paper. At nine-thirty Joseph Loveredge left the house for the office of the old-established journal of which he was the incorruptible and honoured City editor. At one-forty-five, having left his office at one-thirty, Joseph Loveredge entered the Autolycus Club and sat down to lunch. Everything else in Joseph's life was arranged with similar preciseness, so far as was possible with the duties of a City editor. Monday evening Joseph spent with musical friends at Brixton. Friday was Joseph's theatre night. On Tuesdays and Thursdays he was open to receive invitations out to dinner; on Wednesdays and Saturdays he invited four friends to dine with him at Regent's Park. On Sundays, whatever the season, Joseph Loveredge took an excursion into the country. He had his regular hours for reading, his regular hours for thinking. Whether in Fleet Street, or the Tyrol, on the Thames, or in the Vatican, you might recognise him from afar by his grey frock-coat, his patent-leather boots, his brown felt hat, his lavender tie. The man was a born bachelor. When the news of his engagement crept through the smoky portals of the Autolycus Club nobody believed it.

"Impossible!" asserted Jack Herring. "I've known Joey's life for fifteen years. Every five minutes is arranged for. He could never have found the time to do it."

"He doesn't like women, not in that way; I've heard him say so," explained Alexander the Poet. "His opinion is that women are the artists of Society—delightful as entertainers, but troublesome to live with."

"I call to mind," said the Wee Laddie, "a story he told me in this verra room, barely three months agone: Some half a dozen of them were gong home together from the Devonshire. They had had a joyous evening, and one of them—Joey did not notice which—suggested their dropping in at his place just for a final whisky. They were laughing and talking in the dining-room, when their hostess suddenly appeared upon the scene in a costume—so Joey described it—the charm of which was its variety. She was a nice-looking woman, Joey said, but talked too much; and when the first lull occurred, Joey turned to the man sitting nighest to him, and who looked bored, and suggested in a whisper that it was about time they went.

"'Perhaps you had better go,' assented the bored-looking man. 'Wish I could come with you; but, you see, I live here.'"

"I don't believe it," said Somerville the Briefless. "He's been cracking his jokes, and some silly woman has taken him seriously."

But the rumour grew into report, developed detail, lost all charm, expanded into plain recital of fact. Joey had not been seen within the Club for more than a week—in itself a deadly confirmation. The question became: Who was she—what was she like?

"It's none of our set, or we should have heard something from her side before now," argued acutely Somerville the Briefless.

"Some beastly kid who will invite us to dances and forget the supper," feared Johnny Bulstrode, commonly called the Babe. "Old men always fall in love with young girls."

"Forty," explained severely Peter Hope, editor and part proprietor of *Good Humour*, "is not old."

"Well, it isn't young," persisted Johnny.

"Good thing for you, Johnny, if it is a girl," thought Jack Herring. "Somebody for you to play with. I often feel sorry for you, having nobody but grown-up people to talk to."

"They do get a bit stodgy after a certain age," agreed the Babe.

"I am hoping," said Peter, "it will be some sensible, pleasant woman, a little over thirty. He is a dear fellow, Loveredge; and forty is a very good age for a man to marry."

"Well, if I'm not married before I'm forty—" said the Babe.

"Oh, don't you fret," Jack Herring interrupted him—"a pretty boy like you! We will give a ball next season, and bring you out, if you're good—get you off our hands in no time."

It was August. Joey went away for his holiday without again entering the Club. The lady's name was Henrietta Elizabeth Doone. It was said by the *Morning Post* that she was connected with the Doones of Gloucestershire.

Doones of Gloucestershire—Doones of Gloucestershire mused Miss Ramsbotham, Society journalist, who wrote the weekly Letter to Clorinda, discussing the matter with Peter Hope in the editorial office of *Good Humour*. "Knew a Doon who kept a big second-hand store in Euston Road and called himself an auctioneer. He bought a small place in Gloucestershire and added an 'e' to his name. Wonder if it's the same?"

"I had a cat called Elizabeth once," said Peter Hope.

"I don't see what that's got to do with it."

"No, of course not," agreed Peter. "But I was rather fond of it. It was a quaint sort of animal, considered as a cat—would never speak to another cat, and hated being out after ten o'clock at night."

"What happened to it?" demanded Miss Ramsbotham.

"Fell off a roof," sighed Peter Hope. "Wasn't used to them."

The marriage took place abroad, at the English Church at Montreux. Mr. and Mrs. Loveredge returned at the end of

September. The Autolycus Club subscribed to send a present of a punch-bowl, left cards, and waited with curiosity to see the bride. But no invitation arrived. Nor for a month was Joey himself seen within the Club. Then, one foggy afternoon, waking after a doze, with a cold cigar in his mouth, Jack Herring noticed he was not the only occupant of the smoking-room. In a far corner, near a window, sat Joseph Loveredge reading a magazine. Jack Herring rubbed his eyes, then rose and crossed the room.

"I thought at first," explained Jack Herring, recounting the incident later in the evening, "that I must be dreaming. There he sat, drinking his five o'clock whisky-and-soda, the same Joey Loveredge I had known for fifteen years; yet not the same. Not a feature altered, not a hair on his head changed, yet the whole face was different; the same body, the same clothes, but another man. We talked for half an hour; he remembered everything that Joey Loveredge had known. I couldn't understand it. Then, as the clock struck, and he rose, saying he must be home at half-past five, the explanation suddenly occurred to me: *Joey Loveredge was dead; this was a married man.*"

"We don't want your feeble efforts at psychological romance," told him Somerville the Briefless. "We want to know what you talked about. Dead or married, the man who can drink whisky-and-soda must be held responsible for his actions. What's the little beggar mean by cutting us all in this way? Did he ask after any of us? Did he leave any message for any of us? Did he invite any of us to come an see him?"

"Yes, he did ask after nearly everybody; I was coming to that. But he didn't leave any message. I didn't gather that he was pining for old relationships with any of us."

"Well, I shall go round to the office to-morrow morning," said Somerville the Briefless, "and force my way in if necessary. This is getting mysterious."

But Somerville returned only to puzzle the Autolycus Club still further. Joey had talked about the weather, the state of political parties, had received with unfeigned interest all gossip concerning his old friends; but about himself, his wife, nothing had been gleaned. Mrs. Loveredge was well; Mrs. Loveredge's relations were also well. But at present Mrs. Loveredge was not receiving.

Members of the Autolycus Club with time upon their hands took up the business of private detectives. Mrs. Loveredge turned out to be a handsome, well-dressed lady of about thirty, as Peter Hope had desired. At eleven in the morning, Mrs. Loveredge shopped in the neighbourhood of the Hampstead Road. In the afternoon, Mrs. Loveredge, in a hired carriage, would slowly promenade the Park, looking, it was noticed, with intense interest at the occupants of other carriages as they passed, but evidently having no acquaintances among them. The carriage, as a general rule, would call at Joey's office at five, and Mr. and Mrs. Loveredge would drive home. Jack Herring, as the oldest friend, urged by the other members, took the bull by the horns and called boldly. On neither occasion was Mrs. Loveredge at home.

"I'm damned if I go again!" said Jack. "She was in the second time, I know. I watched her into the house. Confound the stuck-up pair of them!"

Bewilderment gave place to indignation. Now and again Joey would creep, a mental shadow of his former self, into the Club where once every member would have risen with a smile to greet him. They gave him curt answers and turned away from him. Peter Hope one afternoon found him there alone, standing with his hands in his pockets looking out of window. Peter was fifty, so he said, maybe a little older; men of forty were to him mere boys. So Peter, who hated mysteries, stepped forward with a determined air and clapped Joey on the shoulder.

"I want to know, Joey," said Peter, "I want to know whether I am to go on liking you, or whether I've got to think poorly of you. Out with it."

Joey turned to him a face so full of misery that Peter's heart was touched. "You can't tell how wretched it makes me," said Joey. "I didn't know it was possible to feel so uncomfortable as I have felt during these last three months."

"It's the wife, I suppose?" suggested Peter.

"She's a dear girl. She only has one fault."

"It's a pretty big one," returned Peter. "I should try and break her of it if I were you."

"Break her of it!" cried the little man. "You might as well advise me to break a brick wall with my head. I had no idea what they were like. I never dreamt it."

"But what is her objection to us? We are clean, we are fairly intelligent—"

"My dear Peter, do you think I haven't said all that, and a hundred things more? A woman! she gets an idea into her head, and every argument against it hammers it in further. She has gained her notion of what she calls Bohemia from the comic journals. It's our own fault, we have done it ourselves. There's no persuading her that it's a libel."

"Won't she see a few of us—judge for herself? There's Porson—why Porson might have been a bishop. Or Somerville—Somerville's Oxford accent is wasted here. It has no chance."

"It isn't only that," explained Joey; "she has ambitions, social ambitions. She thinks that if we begin with the wrong set, we'll never get into the right. We have three friends at present, and, so far as I can see, are never likely to have any more. My dear boy, you'd never believe there could exist such bores. There's a man and his wife named Holyoake. They dine with us on Thursdays, and we dine with them on Tuesdays. Their only title to existence consists in their having a cousin in the House of Lords; they claim no other right themselves. He is a widower, getting on for eighty. Apparently he's the only relative they have, and when he dies, they talk of retiring into the country. There's a fellow named Cutler, who visited once at Marlborough House in connection with a charity. You'd think to listen to him that he had designs upon the throne. The most tiresome of them all is a noisy woman who, as far as I can make out, hasn't any name at all. 'Miss Montgomery' is on her cards, but that is only what she calls herself. Who she really is! It would shake the foundations of European society if known. We sit and talk about the aristocracy; we don't seem to know anybody else. I tried on one occasion a little sarcasm as a corrective—recounted conversations between myself and the Prince of Wales, in which I invariably addressed him as 'Teddy.' It sounds tall, I know, but those people took it in. I was too astonished to undeceive them at the time, the consequence is I am a sort of little god to them. They come round me and ask for more. What am I to do? I am helpless among them. I've never had anything to do before with the really first-prize idiot; the usual type, of course, one knows, but these, if you haven't met them, are inconceivable. I try insulting them; they don't even know I am insulting them. Short of dragging them out of their chairs and kicking them round the room, I don't see how to make them understand it."

"And Mrs. Loveredge?" asked the sympathetic Peter, "is she—"

"Between ourselves," said Joey, sinking his voice to a needless whisper, seeing he and Peter were the sole occupants of the smoking-room—"I couldn't, of course, say it to a younger man—but between ourselves, my wife is a charming woman. You don't know her."

"Doesn't seem much chance of my ever doing so," laughed Peter.

"So graceful, so dignified, so—so queenly," continued the little man, with rising enthusiasm. "She has only one fault—she has no sense of humour."

To Peter, as it has been said, men of forty were mere boys.

"My dear fellow, whatever could have induced you—"

"I know—I know all that," interrupted the mere boy. "Nature arranges it on purpose. Tall and solemn prigs marry little women with turned-up noses. Cheerful little fellows like myself—we marry serious, stately women. If it were otherwise, the human race would be split up into species."

"Of course, if you were actuated by a sense of public duty—"

"Don't be a fool, Peter Hope," returned the little man. "I'm in love with my wife just as she is, and always shall be. I know the woman with a sense of humour, and of the two I prefer the one without. The Juno type is my ideal. I must take the rough with the smooth. One can't have a jolly, chirpy Juno, and wouldn't care for her if one could."

"Then are you going to give up all your old friends?"

"Don't suggest it," pleaded the little man. "You don't know how miserable it makes me—the mere idea. Tell them to be patient. The secret of dealing with women, I have found, is to do nothing rashly." The clock struck five. "I must go now," said Joey. "Don't misjudge her, Peter, and don't let the others. She's a dear girl. You'll like her, all of you, when you know her. A dear girl! She only has that one fault."

Joey went out.

Peter did his best that evening to explain the true position of affairs without imputing snobbery to Mrs. Loveredge. It was a difficult task, and Peter cannot be said to have accomplished it successfully. Anger and indignation against Joey gave place to pity. The members of the Autolycus Club also experienced a little irritation on their own account.

"What does the woman take us for?" demanded Somerville the Briefless. "Doesn't she know that we lunch with real actors and actresses, that once a year we are invited to dine at the Mansion House?"

"Has she never heard of the aristocracy of genius?" demanded Alexander the Poet.

"The explanation may be that possibly she has seen it," feared the Wee Laddie.

"One of us ought to waylay the woman," argued the Babe—"insist upon her talking to him for ten minutes. I've half a mind to do it myself."

Jack Herring said nothing—seemed thoughtful.

The next morning Jack Herring, still thoughtful, called at the editorial offices of *Good Humour*, in Crane Court, and borrowed Miss Ramsbotham's Debrett. Three days later Jack Herring informed the Club casually that he had dined the night before with Mr. and Mrs. Loveredge. The Club gave Jack Herring politely to understand that they regarded him as a liar, and proceeded to demand particulars.

"If I wasn't there," explained Jack Herring, with unanswerable logic, "how can I tell you anything about it?"

This annoyed the Club, whose curiosity had been whetted. Three members, acting in the interests of the whole, solemnly undertook to believe whatever he might tell them. But Jack Herring's feelings had been wounded.

"When gentlemen cast a doubt upon another gentleman's veracity—"

"We didn't cast a doubt," explained Somerville the Briefless. "We merely said that we personally did not believe you. We didn't say we couldn't believe you; it is a case for individual effort. If you give us particulars bearing the impress of reality, supported by details that do not unduly contradict each other, we are prepared to put aside our natural suspicions and face the possibility of your statement being correct."

"It was foolish of me," said Jack Herring. "I thought perhaps it would amuse you to hear what sort of a woman Mrs. Loveredge was like—some description of Mrs. Loveredge's uncle. Miss Montgomery, friend of Mrs. Loveredge, is certainly one of the most remarkable women I have ever met. Of course, that isn't her real name. But, as I have said, it was foolish of me. These people—you will never meet them, you will never see them; of what interest can they be to you?"

"They had forgotten to draw down the blinds, and he climbed up a lamp-post and looked through the window," was the solution of the problem put forward by the Wee Laddie.

"I'm dining there again on Saturday," volunteered Jack Herring. "If any of you will promise not to make a disturbance, you can hang about on the Park side, underneath the shadow of the fence, and watch me go in. My hansom will draw up at the door within a few minutes of eight."

The Babe and the Poet agreed to undertake the test.

"You won't mind our hanging round a little while, in case you're thrown out again?" asked the Babe.

"Not in the least, so far as I am concerned," replied Jack Herring. "Don't leave it too late and make your mother anxious."

"It's true enough," the Babe recounted afterwards. "The door was opened by a manservant and he went straight in. We walked up and down for half an hour, and unless they put him out the back way, he's telling the truth."

"Did you hear him give his name?" asked Somerville, who was stroking his moustache.

"No, we were too far off," explained the Babe. "But—I'll swear it was Jack—there couldn't be any mistake about that."

"Perhaps not," agreed Somerville the Briefless.

Somerville the Briefless called at the offices of *Good Humour*, in Crane Court, the following morning, and he also borrowed Miss Ramsbotham's Debrett.

"What's the meaning of it?" demanded the sub-editor.

"Meaning of what?"

"This sudden interest of all you fellows in the British Peerage."

"All of us?"

"Well, Herring was here last week, poring over that book for half an hour, with the *Morning Post* spread out before him. Now you're doing the same thing."

"Ah! Jack Herring, was he? I thought as much. Don't talk about it, Tommy. I'll tell you later on."

On the following Monday, the Briefless one announced to the Club that he had received an invitation to dine at the Loveredges' on the following Wednesday. On Tuesday, the Briefless one entered the Club with a slow and stately step. Halting opposite old Goslin the porter, who had emerged from his box with the idea of discussing the Oxford and Cambridge boat race, Somerville, removing his hat with a sweep of the arm, held it out in silence. Old Goslin, much astonished, took it mechanically, whereupon the Briefless one, shaking himself free from his Inverness cape, flung it lightly after the hat, and strolled on, not noticing that old Goslin, unaccustomed to coats lightly and elegantly thrown at him, dropping the hat, had caught it on his head, and had been, in the language of the prompt-book, "left struggling." The Briefless one, entering the smoking-room, lifted a chair and let it fall again with a crash, and sitting down upon it, crossed his legs and rang the bell.

"Ye're doing it verra weel," remarked approvingly the Wee Laddie. "Ye're just fitted for it by nature."

"Fitted for what?" demanded the Briefless one, waking up apparently from a dream.

"For an Adelphi guest at eighteenpence the night," assured him the Wee Laddie. "Ye're just splendid at it."

The Briefless one, muttering that the worst of mixing with journalists was that if you did not watch yourself, you fell into their ways, drank his whisky in silence. Later, the Babe swore on a copy of *Sell's Advertising Guide* that, crossing the Park, he had seen the Briefless one leaning over the railings of Rotten Row, clad in a pair of new kid gloves, swinging a silver-headed cane.

One morning towards the end of the week, Joseph Loveredge, looking twenty years younger than when Peter had last seen him, dropped in at the editorial office of *Good Humour* and demanded of Peter Hope how he felt and what he thought of the present price of Emma Mines.

Peter Hope's fear was that the gambling fever was spreading to all classes of society.

"I want you to dine with us on Sunday," said Joseph Loveredge. "Jack Herring will be there. You might bring Tommy with you."

Peter Hope gulped down his astonishment and said he should be delighted; he thought that Tommy also was disengaged. "Mrs. Loveredge out of town, I presume?" questioned Peter Hope.

"On the contrary," replied Joseph Loveredge, "I want you to meet her."

Joseph Loveredge removed a pile of books from one chair and placed them carefully upon another, after which he went and stood before the fire.

"Don't if you don't like," said Joseph Loveredge; "but if you don't mind, you might call yourself, just for the evening—say, the Duke of Warrington."

"Say the what?" demanded Peter Hope.

"The Duke of Warrington," repeated Joey. "We are rather short of dukes. Tommy can be the Lady Adelaide, your daughter."

"Don't be an ass!" said Peter Hope.

"I'm not an ass," assured him Joseph Loveredge. "He is wintering in Egypt. You have run back for a week to attend to business. There is no Lady Adelaide, so that's quite simple."

"But what in the name of—" began Peter Hope.

"Don't you see what I'm driving at?" persisted Joey. "It was Jack's idea at the beginning. I was frightened myself at first, but it is working to perfection. She sees you, and sees that you are a gentleman. When the truth comes out—as, of course, it must later on—the laugh will be against her."

"You think—you think that'll comfort her?" suggested Peter Hope.

"It's the only way, and it is really wonderfully simple. We never mention the aristocracy now—it would be like talking shop. We just enjoy ourselves. You, by the way, I met in connection with the movement for rational dress. You are a bit of a crank, fond of frequenting Bohemian circles."

"I am risking something, I know," continued Joey; "but it's worth it. I couldn't have existed much longer. We go slowly, and are very careful. Jack is Lord Mount-Primrose, who has taken up with anti-vaccination and who never goes out into Society. Somerville is Sir Francis Baldwin, the great authority on centipedes. The Wee Laddie is coming next week as Lord Garrick, who married that dancing-girl, Prissy Something, and started a furniture shop in Bond Street. I had some difficulty at first. She wanted to send out paragraphs, but I explained that was only done by vulgar persons—that when the nobility came to you as friends, it was considered bad taste. She is a dear girl, as I have always told you, with only one fault. A woman easier to deceive one could not wish for. I don't myself see why the truth ever need come out—provided we keep our heads."

"Seems to me you've lost them already," commented Peter; "you're overdoing it."

"The more of us the better," explained Joey; "we help each other. Besides, I particularly want you in it. There's a sort of superior Pickwickian atmosphere surrounding you that disarms suspicion."

"You leave me out of it," growled Peter.

"See here," laughed Joey; "you come as the Duke of Warrington, and bring Tommy with you, and I'll write your City article."

"For how long?" snapped Peter. Incorruptible City editors are not easily picked up.

"Oh, well, for as long as you like."

"On that understanding," agreed Peter, "I'm willing to make a fool of myself in your company."

"You'll soon get used to it," Joey told him; "eight o'clock, then, on Sunday; plain evening dress. If you like to wear a bit of red ribbon in your buttonhole, why, do so. You can get it at Evans', in Covent Garden."

"And Tommy is the Lady—"

"Adelaide. Let her have a taste for literature, then she needn't wear gloves. I know she hates them." Joey turned to go.

"Am I married?" asked Peter.

Joey paused. "I should avoid all reference to your matrimonial affairs if I were you," was Joey's advice. "You didn't come out of that business too well."

"Oh! as bad as that, was I? You don't think Mrs. Loveredge will object to me?"

"I have asked her that. She's a dear, broad-minded girl. I've promised not to leave you alone with Miss Montgomery, and Willis has had instructions not to let you mix your drinks."

"I'd have liked to have been someone a trifle more respectable," grumbled Peter.

"We rather wanted a duke," explained Joey, "and he was the only one that fitted in all round."

The dinner a was a complete success. Tommy, entering into the spirit of the thing, bought a new pair of open-work stockings and assumed a languid drawl. Peter, who was growing forgetful, introduced her as the Lady Alexandra; it did not seem to matter, both beginning with an A. She greeted Lord Mount-Primrose as "Billy," and asked affectionately after his mother. Joey told his raciest stories. The Duke of Warrington called everybody by their Christian names, and seemed well acquainted with Bohemian society—a more amiable nobleman it would have been impossible to discover. The lady whose real name was not Miss Montgomery sat in speechless admiration. The hostess was the personification of gracious devotion.

Other little dinners, equally successful, followed. Joey's acquaintanceship appeared to be confined exclusively to the higher circles of the British aristocracy—with one exception: that of a German baron, a short, stout gentleman, who talked English well, but with an accent, and who, when he desired to be impressive, laid his right forefinger on the right side of his nose and thrust his whole face forward. Mrs. Loveredge wondered why her husband had not introduced them sooner, but was too blissful to be suspicious. The Autolycus Club was gradually changing its tone. Friends could no longer recognise one another by the voice. Every corner had its solitary student practising high-class intonation. Members dropped into the habit of addressing one another as "dear chappie," and, discarding pipes, took to cheap cigars. Many of the older *habitues* resigned.

All might have gone well to the end of time if only Mrs. Loveredge had left all social arrangements in the hands of her husband—had not sought to aid his efforts. To a certain political garden-party, one day in the height of the season, were invited Joseph Loveredge and Mrs. Joseph Loveredge, his wife. Mr. Joseph Loveredge at the last moment found himself unable to attend. Mrs. Joseph Loveredge went alone, met there various members of the British aristocracy. Mrs. Joseph Loveredge, accustomed to friendship with the aristocracy, felt at her ease and was natural and agreeable. The wife of an eminent peer talked to her and liked her. It occurred to Mrs. Joseph Loveredge that this lady might be induced to visit her house in Regent's Park, there to mingle with those of her own class.

"Lord Mount-Primrose, the Duke of Warrington, and a few others will be dining with us on Sunday next," suggested Mrs. Loveredge. "Will not you do us the honour of coming? We are, of course, only simple folk ourselves, but somehow people seem to like us."

The wife of the eminent peer looked at Mrs. Loveredge, looked round the grounds, looked at Mrs. Loveredge again, and said she would like to come. Mrs. Joseph Loveredge intended at first to tell her husband of her success, but a little devil entering into her head and whispering to her that it would be amusing, she resolved to keep it as a surprise, to be sprung upon him at eight o'clock on Sunday. The surprise proved all she could have hoped for.

The Duke of Warrington, having journalistic matters to discuss with Joseph Loveredge, arrived at half-past seven, wearing on his shirt-front a silver star, purchased in Eagle Street the day before for eight-and-six. There accompanied him the Lady Alexandra, wearing the identical ruby necklace that every night for the past six months, and twice on Saturdays, "John Strongheart" had been falsely accused of stealing. Lord Garrick, having picked up his wife (Miss Ramsbotham) outside the Mother Redcap, arrived with her on foot at a quarter to eight. Lord Mount-Primrose, together with Sir Francis Baldwin, dashed up in a hansom at seven-fifty. His Lordship, having lost the toss, paid the fare. The Hon. Harry Sykes (commonly called "the Babe") was ushered in five minutes later. The noble company assembled in the drawing-room chatted blithely while waiting for dinner to be announced. The Duke of Warrington was telling an anecdote about a cat, which nobody appeared to believe. Lord Mount-Primrose desired to know whether by any chance it might be the same animal that every night at half-past nine had been in the habit of climbing up his Grace's railings and knocking at his Grace's door. The Honourable Harry was saying that, speaking of cats, he once had a sort of terrier—when the door was thrown open and Willis announced the Lady Mary Sutton.

Mr. Joseph Loveredge, who was sitting near the fire, rose up. Lord Mount-Primrose, who was standing near the piano, sat down. The Lady Mary Sutton paused in the doorway. Mrs. Loveredge crossed the room to greet her.

"Let me introduce you to my husband," said Mrs. Loveredge. "Joey, my dear, the Lady Mary Sutton. I met the Lady Mary at the O'Meyers' the other day, and she was good enough to accept my invitation. I forgot to tell you."

Mr. Loveredge said he was delighted; after which, although as a rule a chatty man, he seemed to have nothing else to say. And a silence fell.

Somerville the Briefless—till then. That evening has always been reckoned the starting-point of his career. Up till then nobody thought he had much in him—walked up and held out his hand.

"You don't remember me, Lady Mary," said the Briefless one. "I met you some years ago; we had a most interesting conversation— Sir Francis Baldwin."

The Lady Mary stood for a moment trying apparently to recollect. She was a handsome, fresh-complexioned woman of about forty, with frank, agreeable eyes. The Lady Mary glanced at Lord

Garrick, who was talking rapidly to Lord Mount-Primrose, who was not listening, and who could not have understood even if he had been, Lord Garrick, without being aware of it, having dropped into broad Scotch. From him the Lady Mary glanced at her hostess, and from her hostess to her host.

The Lady Mary took the hand held out to her. "Of course," said the Lady Mary; "how stupid of me! It was the day of my own wedding, too. You really must forgive me. We talked of quite a lot of things. I remember now."

Mrs. Loveredge, who prided herself upon maintaining old-fashioned courtesies, proceeded to introduce the Lady Mary to her fellow-guests, a little surprised that her ladyship appeared to know so few of them. Her ladyship's greeting of the Duke of Warrington was accompanied, it was remarked, by a somewhat curious smile. To the Duke of Warrington's daughter alone did the Lady Mary address remark.

"My dear," said the Lady Mary, "how you have grown since last we met!"

The announcement of dinner, as everybody felt, came none too soon.

It was not a merry feast. Joey told but one story; he told it three times, and twice left out the point. Lord Mount-Primrose took sifted sugar with *pate de foie gras* and ate it with a spoon. Lord Garrick, talking a mixture of Scotch and English, urged his wife to give up housekeeping and take a flat in Gower Street, which, as he pointed out, was central. She could have her meals sent in to her and so avoid all trouble. The Lady Alexandra's behaviour appeared to Mrs. Loveredge not altogether well-bred. An eccentric young noblewoman Mrs. Loveredge had always found her, but wished on this occasion that she had been a little less eccentric. Every few minutes the Lady Alexandra buried her face in her serviette, and shook and rocked, emitting stifled sounds, apparently those of acute physical pain. Mrs. Loveredge hoped she was not feeling ill, but the Lady Alexandra appeared incapable of coherent reply. Twice during the meal the Duke of Warrington rose from the table and began wandering round the room; on each occasion, asked what he wanted, had replied meekly that he was merely looking for his snuff-box, and had sat down again. The only person who seemed to enjoy the dinner was the Lady Mary Sutton.

The ladies retired upstairs into the drawing-room. Mrs. Lover-edge, breaking a long silence, remarked it as unusual that no sound of merriment reached them from the dining-room. The explanation was that the entire male portion of the party, on being left to themselves, had immediately and in a body crept on tiptoe into Joey's study, which, fortunately, happened to be on the ground floor. Joey, unlocking the bookcase, had taken out his Debrett, but appeared incapable of understanding it. Sir Francis Baldwin had taken it from his unresisting hands; the remaining aristocracy huddled themselves into a corner and waited in silence.

"I think I've got it all clearly," announced Sir Francis Baldwin, after five minutes, which to the others had been an hour. "Yes, I don't think I'm making any mistake. She's the daughter of the Duke of Truro, married in '53 the Duke of Warrington, at St. Peter's, Eaton Square; gave birth in '55 to a daughter, the Lady Grace Alexandra Warberton Sutton, which makes the child just thirteen. In '63 divorced the Duke of Warrington. Lord Mount-Primrose, so far as I can make out, must be her second cousin. I appear to have married her in '66 at Hastings. It doesn't seem to me that we could have got together a homelier little party to meet her even if we had wanted to."

Nobody spoke; nobody had anything particularly worth saying. The door opened, and the Lady Alexandra (otherwise Tommy) entered the room.

"Isn't it time," suggested the Lady Alexandra, "that some of you came upstairs?"

"I was thinking myself," explained Joey, the host, with a grim smile, "it was about time that I went out and drowned myself. The canal is handy."

"Put it off till to-morrow," Tommy advised him. "I have asked her ladyship to give me a lift home, and she has promised to do so. She is evidently a woman with a sense of humour. Wait till after I have had a talk with her."

Six men, whispering at the same time, were prepared with advice; but Tommy was not taking advice.

"Come upstairs, all of you," insisted Tommy, "and make yourselves agreeable. She's going in a quarter of an hour."

Six silent men, the host leading, the two husbands bringing up the rear, ascended the stairs, each with the sensation of being twice his usual weight. Six silent men entered the drawing-room and sat down on chairs. Six silent men tried to think of something interesting to say.

Miss Ramsbotham—it was that or hysterics, as she afterwards explained—stifling a sob, opened the piano. But the only thing she could remember was "Champagne Charlie is my Name," a song then popular in the halls. Five men, when she had finished, begged her to go on. Miss Ramsbotham, speaking in a shrill falsetto, explained it was the only tune she knew. Four of them begged her to play it again. Miss Ramsbotham played it a second time with involuntary variations.

The Lady Mary's carriage was announced by the imperturbable Willis. The party, with the exception of the Lady Mary and the hostess, suppressed with difficulty an inclination to burst into a cheer. The Lady Mary thanked Mrs. Loveredge for a most interesting evening, and beckoned Tommy to accompany her. With her disappearance, a wild hilarity, uncanny in its suddenness, took possession of the remaining guests.

A few days later, the Lady Mary's carriage again drew up before the little house in Regent's Park. Mrs. Loveredge, fortunately, was at home. The carriage remained waiting for quite a long time. Mrs. Loveredge, after it was gone, locked herself in her own room. The under-housemaid reported to the kitchen that, passing the door, she had detected sounds indicative of strong emotion.

Through what ordeal Joseph Loveredge passed was never known. For a few weeks the Autolycus Club missed him. Then gradually, as aided by Time they have a habit of doing, things righted themselves. Joseph Loveredge received his old friends; his friends received Joseph Loveredge. Mrs. Loveredge, as a hostess, came to have only one failing—a marked coldness of demeanour towards all people with titles, whenever introduced to her.

STORY THE SIXTH

"The Babe" Applies for Shares

PEOPLE said of the new journal, *Good Humour*—people of taste and judgment, that it was the brightest, the cleverest, the most literary penny weekly that ever had been offered to the public. This made Peter Hope, editor and part-proprietor, very happy. William Clodd, business manager, and also part-proprietor, it left less elated.

"Must be careful," said William Clodd, "that we don't make it too clever. Happy medium, that's the ideal."

People said—people of taste and judgment, that *Good Humour* was more worthy of support than all the other penny weeklies put together. People of taste and judgment even went so far, some of them, as to buy it. Peter Hope, looking forward, saw fame and fortune coming to him.

William Clodd, looking round about him, said—

"Doesn't it occur to you, Guv'nor, that we're getting this thing just a trifle too high class?"

"What makes you think that?" demanded Peter Hope.

"Our circulation, for one thing," explained Clodd. "The returns for last month—"

"I'd rather you didn't mention them, if you don't mind," interrupted Peter Hope; "somehow, hearing the actual figures always depresses me."

"Can't say I feel inspired by them myself," admitted Clodd.

"It will come," said Peter Hope, "it will come in time. We must educate the public up to our level."

"If there is one thing, so far as I have noticed," said William Clodd, "that the public are inclined to pay less for than another, it is for being educated."

"What are we to do?" asked Peter Hope.

"What you want," answered William Clodd, "is an office-boy."

"How will our having an office-boy increase our circulation?" demanded Peter Hope. "Besides, it was agreed that we could do without one for the first year. Why suggest more expense?"

"I don't mean an ordinary office-boy," explained Clodd. "I mean the sort of boy that I rode with in the train going down to Stratford yesterday."

"What was there remarkable about him?"

"Nothing. He was reading the current number of the *Penny Novelist*. Over two hundred thousand people buy it. He is one of them. He told me so. When he had done with it, he drew from his pocket a copy of the *Halfpenny Joker*—they guarantee a circulation of seventy thousand. He sat and chuckled over it until we got to Bow."

"But—"

"You wait a minute. I'm coming to the explanation. That boy represents the reading public. I talked to him. The papers he likes best are the papers that have the largest sales. He never made a single mistake. The others—those of them he had seen—he dismissed as 'rot.' What he likes is what the great mass of the journal-buying public likes. Please him—I took his name and address, and he is willing to come to us for eight shillings a week—and you please the people that buy. Not the people that glance through a paper when it is lying on the smoking-room table, and tell you it is damned good, but the people that plank down their penny. That's the sort we want."

Peter Hope, able editor, with ideals, was shocked—indignant. William Clodd, business man, without ideals, talked figures.

"There's the advertiser to be thought of," persisted Clodd. "I don't pretend to be a George Washington, but what's the use of telling lies that sound like lies, even to one's self while one's telling them? Give me a genuine sale of twenty thousand, and I'll undertake, without committing myself, to convey an impression of forty. But when the actual figures are under eight thousand—well, it hampers you, if you happen to have a conscience.

"Give them every week a dozen columns of good, sound literature," continued Clodd insinuatingly, "but wrap it up in twenty-four columns of jam. It's the only way they'll take it, and you will be doing them good—educating them without their knowing it. All powder and no jam! Well, they don't open their mouths, that's all."

Clodd was a man who knew how to get his way. Flipp—spelled Philip—Tweetel arrived in due course of time at 23, Crane Court, ostensibly to take up the position of *Good Humour's* office-boy; in reality, and without his being aware of it, to act as its literary taster. Stories in which Flipp became absorbed were accepted. Peter groaned, but contented himself with correcting only their grosser grammatical blunders; the experiment should be tried in all good faith. Humour at which Flipp laughed was printed. Peter tried to ease his conscience by increasing his subscription to the fund for destitute compositors, but only partially succeeded. Poetry that brought a tear to the eye of Flipp was given leaded type. People of taste and judgment said *Good Humour* had disappointed them. Its circulation, slowly but steadily, increased.

"See!" cried the delighted Clodd; "told you so!"

"It's sad to think—" began Peter.

"Always is," interrupted Clodd cheerfully. "Moral—don't think too much."

"Tell you what we'll do," added Clodd. "We'll make a fortune out of this paper. Then when we can afford to lose a little money, we'll launch a paper that shall appeal only to the intellectual portion of the public. Meanwhile—"

A squat black bottle with a label attached, standing on the desk, arrested Clodd's attention.

"When did this come?" asked Clodd.

"About an hour ago," Peter told him.

"Any order with it?"

"I think so." Peter searched for and found a letter addressed to "William Clodd, Esq., Advertising Manager, *Good Humour.*" Clodd tore it open, hastily devoured it.

"Not closed up yet, are you?"

"No, not till eight o'clock."

"Good! I want you to write me a par. Do it now, then you won't forget it. For the 'Walnuts and Wine' column."

Peter sat down, headed a sheet of paper: 'For W. and W. Col.'

"What is it?" questioned Peter—"something to drink?"

"It's a sort of port," explained Clodd, "that doesn't get into your head."

"You consider that an advantage?" queried Peter.

"Of course. You can drink more of it."

Peter continued to write: 'Possesses all the qualities of an old vintage port, without those deleterious properties—' "I haven't tasted it, Clodd," hinted Peter.

"That's all right—I have."

"And was it good?"

"Splendid stuff. Say it's 'delicious and invigorating.' They'll be sure to quote that."

Peter wrote on: 'Personally I have found it delicious and—' Peter left off writing. "I really think, Clodd, I ought to taste it. You see, I am personally recommending it."

"Finish that par. Let me have it to take round to the printers. Then put the bottle in your pocket. Take it home and make a night of it."

Clodd appeared to be in a mighty hurry. Now, this made Peter only the more suspicious. The bottle was close to his hand. Clodd tried to intercept him, but was not quick enough.

"You're not used to temperance drinks," urged Clodd. "Your palate is not accustomed to them."

"I can tell whether it's 'delicious' or not, surely?" pleaded Peter, who had pulled out the cork.

"It's a quarter-page advertisement for thirteen weeks. Put it down and don't be a fool!" urged Clodd.

"I'm going to put it down," laughed Peter, who was fond of his joke. Peter poured out half a tumblerful, and drank—some of it.

"Like it?" demanded Clodd, with a savage grin.

"You are sure—you are sure it was the right bottle?" gasped Peter.

"Bottle's all right," Clodd assured him. "Try some more. Judge it fairly."

Peter ventured on another sip. "You don't think they would be satisfied if I recommended it as a medicine?" insinuated Peter— "something to have about the house in case of accidental poisoning?"

"Better go round and suggest the idea to them yourself. I've done with it." Clodd took up his hat.

"I'm sorry—I'm very sorry," sighed Peter. "But I couldn't conscientiously—"

Clodd put down his hat again with a bang. "Oh! confound that conscience of yours! Don't it ever think of your creditors? What's the use of my working out my lungs for you, when all you do is to hamper me at every step?"

"Wouldn't it be better policy," urged Peter, "to go for the better class of advertiser, who doesn't ask you for this sort of thing?"

"Go for him!" snorted Clodd. "Do you think I don't go for him? They are just sheep. Get one, you get the lot. Until you've got the one, the others won't listen to you."

"That's true," mused Peter. "I spoke to Wilkinson, of Kingsley's, myself. He advised me to try and get Landor's. He thought that if I could get an advertisement out of Landor, he might persuade his people to give us theirs."

"And if you had gone to Landor, he would have promised you theirs provided you got Kingsley's."

"They will come," thought hopeful Peter. "We are going up steadily. They will come with a rush."

"They had better come soon," thought Clodd. "The only things coming with a rush just now are bills."

"Those articles of young McTear's attracted a good deal of attention," expounded Peter. "He has promised to write me another series."

"Jowett is the one to get hold of," mused Clodd. "Jowett, all the others follow like a flock of geese waddling after the old gander. If only we could get hold of Jowett, the rest would be easy."

Jowett was the proprietor of the famous Marble Soap. Jowett spent on advertising every year a quarter of a million, it was said. Jowett was the stay and prop of periodical literature. New papers that secured the Marble Soap advertisement lived and prospered; the new paper to which it was denied languished and died. Jowett, and how to get hold of him; Jowett, and how to get round him, formed the chief topic of discussion at the council-board of most new papers, *Good Humour* amongst the number.

"I have heard," said Miss Ramsbotham, who wrote the Letter to Clorinda that filled each week the last two pages of *Good Humour*, and that told Clorinda, who lived secluded in the country, the daily history of the highest class society, among whom Miss Ramsbotham appeared to live and have her being; who they were, and what they wore, the wise and otherwise things they did—"I have heard," said Miss Ramsbotham one morning, Jowett being as usual the subject under debate, "that the old man is susceptible to female influence."

"What I have always thought," said Clodd. "A lady advertising-agent might do well. At all events, they couldn't kick her out."

"They might in the end," thought Peter. "Female door-porters would become a profession for muscular ladies if ever the idea took root."

"The first one would get a good start, anyhow," thought Clodd.

The sub-editor had pricked up her ears. Once upon a time, long ago, the sub-editor had succeeded, when all other London journalists had failed, in securing an interview with a certain great statesman. The sub-editor had never forgotten this—nor allowed anyone else to forget it.

"I believe I could get it for you," said the sub-editor.

The editor and the business-manager both spoke together. They spoke with decision and with emphasis.

"Why not?" said the sub-editor. "When nobody else could get at him, it was I who interviewed Prince—"

"We've heard all about that," interrupted the business-manager. "If I had been your father at the time, you would never have done it."

"How could I have stopped her?" retorted Peter Hope. "She never said a word to me."

"You could have kept an eye on her."

"Kept an eye on her! When you've got a girl of your own, you'll know more about them."

"When I have," asserted Clodd, "I'll manage her."

"We know all about bachelor's children," sneered Peter Hope, the editor.

"You leave it to me. I'll have it for you before the end of the week," crowed the sub-editor.

"If you do get it," returned Clodd, "I shall throw it out, that's all."

"You said yourself a lady advertising-agent would be a good idea," the sub-editor reminded him.

"So she might be," returned Clodd; "but she isn't going to be you."

"Why not?"

"Because she isn't, that's why."

"But if—"

"See you at the printer's at twelve," said Clodd to Peter, and went out suddenly.

"Well, I think he's an idiot," said the sub-editor.

"I do not often," said the editor, "but on this point I agree with him. Cadging for advertisements isn't a woman's work."

"But what is the difference between—"

"All the difference in the world," thought the editor.

"You don't know what I was going to say," returned his sub.

"I know the drift of it," asserted the editor.

"But you let me—"

"I know I do—a good deal too much. I'm going to turn over a new leaf."

"All I propose to do—"

"Whatever it is, you're not going to do it," declared the chief. "Shall be back at half-past twelve, if anybody comes."

"It seems to me—" But Peter was gone.

"Just like them all," wailed the sub-editor. "They can't argue; when you explain things to them, they go out. It does make me so mad!"

Miss Ramsbotham laughed. "You are a downtrodden little girl, Tommy."

"As if I couldn't take care of myself!" Tommy's chin was high up in the air.

"Cheer up," suggested Miss Ramsbotham. "Nobody ever tells me not to do anything. I would change with you if I could."

"I'd have walked into that office and have had that advertisement out of old Jowett in five minutes, I know I would," bragged Tommy. "I can always get on with old men."

"Only with the old ones?" queried Miss Ramsbotham.

The door opened. "Anybody in?" asked the face of Johnny Bulstrode, appearing in the jar.

"Can't you see they are?" snapped Tommy.

"Figure of speech," explained Johnny Bulstrode, commonly called "the Babe," entering and closing the door behind him.

"What do you want?" demanded the sub-editor.

"Nothing in particular," replied the Babe.

"Wrong time of the day to come for it, half-past eleven in the morning," explained the sub-editor.

"What's the matter with you?" asked the Babe.

"Feeling very cross," confessed the sub-editor.

The childlike face of the Babe expressed sympathetic inquiry.

"We are very indignant," explained Miss Ramsbotham, "because we are not allowed to rush off to Cannon Street and coax an advertisement out of old Jowett, the soap man. We feel sure that if we only put on our best hat, he couldn't possibly refuse us."

"No coaxing required," thought the sub-editor. "Once get in to see the old fellow and put the actual figures before him, he would clamour to come in."

"Won't he see Clodd?" asked the Babe.

"Won't see anybody on behalf of anything new just at present, apparently," answered Miss Ramsbotham. "It was my fault. I was foolish enough to repeat that I had heard he was susceptible to female charm. They say it was Mrs. Sarkitt that got the advertisement for *The Lamp* out of him. But, of course, it may not be true."

"Wish I was a soap man and had got advertisements to give away," sighed the Babe.

"Wish you were," agreed the sub-editor.

"You should have them all, Tommy."

"My name," corrected him the sub-editor, "is Miss Hope."

"I beg your pardon," said the Babe. "I don't know how it is, but one gets into the way of calling you Tommy."

"I will thank you," said the sub-editor, "to get out of it."

"I am sorry," said the Babe.

"Don't let it occur again," said the sub-editor.

The Babe stood first on one leg and then on the other, but nothing seemed to come of it. "Well," said the Babe, "I just looked in, that's all. Nothing I can do for you?"

"Nothing," thanked him the sub-editor.

"Good morning," said the Babe.

"Good morning," said the sub-editor.

The childlike face of the Babe wore a chastened expression as it slowly descended the stairs. Most of the members of the Autolycus Club looked in about once a day to see if they could do anything for Tommy. Some of them had luck. Only the day before, Porson—a heavy, most uninteresting man—had been sent down all the way to Plaistow to inquire after the wounded hand of a machine-boy. Young Alexander, whose poetry some people could not even understand, had been commissioned to search London for a second-hand edition of Maitland's *Architecture*. Since a fortnight nearly now, when he had been sent out to drive away an organ that would not go, Johnny had been given nothing.

Johnny turned the corner into Fleet Street feeling bitter with his lot. A boy carrying a parcel stumbled against him.

"Beg yer pardon—" the small boy looked up into Johnny's face, "miss," added the small boy, dodging the blow and disappearing into the crowd.

The Babe, by reason of his childlike face, was accustomed to insults of this character, but to-day it especially irritated him. Why at twenty-two could he not grow even a moustache? Why was he only five feet five and a half? Why had Fate cursed him with a pink-and-white complexion, so that the members of his own club had nicknamed him "the Babe," while street-boys as they passed pleaded with him for a kiss? Why was his very voice, a flute-like alto, more suitable—Suddenly an idea sprang to life within his brain. The idea grew. Passing a barber's shop, Johnny went in.

"'Air cut, sir?" remarked the barber, fitting a sheet round Johnny's neck.

"No, shave," corrected Johnny.

"Beg pardon," said the barber, substituting a towel for the sheet. "Do you shave up, sir?" later demanded the barber.

"Yes," answered Johnny.

"Pleasant weather we are having," said the barber.

"Very," assented Johnny.

From the barber's, Johnny went to Stinchcombe's, the costumier's, in Drury Lane.

"I am playing in a burlesque," explained the Babe. "I want you to rig me out completely as a modern girl."

"Peeth o' luck!" said the shopman. "Goth the very bundle for you. Juth come in."

"I shall want everything," explained the Babe, "from the boots to the hat; stays, petticoats—the whole bag of tricks."

"Regular troutheau there," said the shopman, emptying out the canvas bag upon the counter. "Thry 'em on."

The Babe contented himself with trying on the costume and the boots. "Juth made for you!" said the shopman.

A little loose about the chest, suggested the Babe.

"Thath's all right," said the shopman. "Couple o' thmall tow-elths, all thath's wanted."

"You don't think it too showy?" queried the Babe.

"Thowy? Sthylish, thath's all."

"You are sure everything's here?"

"Everythinkth there. 'Thept the bit o' meat inthide," assured him the shopman.

The Babe left a deposit, and gave his name and address. The shopman promised the things should be sent round within an hour. The Babe, who had entered into the spirit of the thing, bought a pair of gloves and a small reticule, and made his way to Bow Street.

"I want a woman's light brown wig," said the Babe to Mr. Cox, the perruquier.

Mr. Cox tried on two. The deceptive appearance of the second Mr. Cox pronounced as perfect.

"Looks more natural on you than your own hair, blessed if it doesn't!" said Mr. Cox.

The wig also was promised within the hour. The spirit of completeness descended upon the Babe. On his way back to his lodgings in Great Queen Street, he purchased a ladylike umbrella and a veil.

Now, a quarter of an hour after Johnny Bulstrode had made his exit by the door of Mr. Stinchcombe's shop, one, Harry Bennett, actor and member of the Autolycus Club, pushed it open and entered. The shop was empty. Harry Bennett hammered with his stick and waited. A piled-up bundle of clothes lay upon the counter; a sheet of paper, with a name and address scrawled across it, rested on the bundle. Harry Bennett, given to idle curiosity, approached and read the same. Harry Bennett, with his stick, poked the bundle, scattering its items over the counter.

"Donth do thath!" said the shopman, coming up. "Juth been putting 'em together."

"What the devil," said Harry Bennett, "is Johnny Bulstrode going to do with that rig-out?"

"How thoud I know?" answered the shopman. "Private theathricals, I suppoth. Friend o' yourth?"

"Yes," replied Harry Bennett. "By Jove! he ought to make a good girl. Should like to see it!"

"Well arthk him for a ticket. Donth make 'em dirty," suggested the shopman.

"I must," said Harry Bennett, and talked about his own affairs.

The rig-out and the wig did not arrive at Johnny's lodgings within the hour as promised, but arrived there within three hours, which was as much as Johnny had expected. It took Johnny nearly an hour to dress, but at last he stood before the plate-glass panel of the wardrobe transformed. Johnny had reason to be pleased with the result. A tall, handsome girl looked back at him out of the glass—a little showily dressed, perhaps, but decidedly *chic*.

"Wonder if I ought to have a cloak," mused Johnny, as a ray of sunshine, streaming through the window, fell upon the image in the glass. "Well, anyhow, I haven't," thought Johnny, as the sunlight died away again, "so it's no good thinking about it."

Johnny seized his reticule and his umbrella and opened cautiously the door. Outside all was silent. Johnny stealthily descended; in the passage paused again. Voices sounded from the basement. Feeling like an escaped burglar, Johnny slipped the latch of the big door and peeped out. A policeman, pasting, turned and looked at him. Johnny hastily drew back and closed the door again. Somebody was ascending from the kitchen. Johnny, caught between two terrors, nearer to the front door than to the stairs, having no time, chose the street. It seemed to Johnny that the street was making for him. A woman came hurriedly towards him. What was she going to say to him? What should he answer her? To his surprise she passed him, hardly noticing him. Wondering what miracle had saved him, he took a few steps forward. A couple of young clerks coming up from behind turned to look at him, but on encountering his answering stare of angry alarm, appeared confused and went their way. It began to dawn upon him that mankind was less discerning than he had feared. Gaining courage as he proceeded, he reached Holborn. Here the larger crowd swept around him indifferent.

"I beg your pardon," said Johnny, coming into collision with a stout gentleman.

"My fault," replied the stout gentleman, as, smiling, he picked up his damaged hat.

"I beg your pardon," repeated Johnny again two minutes later, colliding with a tall young lady.

"Should advise you to take something for that squint of yours," remarked the tall young lady with severity.

"What's the matter with me?" thought Johnny. "Seems to be a sort of mist—" The explanation flashed across him. "Of course," said Johnny to himself, "it's this confounded veil!"

Johnny decided to walk to the Marble Soap offices. "I'll be more used to the hang of things by the time I get there if I walk," thought Johnny. "Hope the old beggar's in."

In Newgate Street, Johnny paused and pressed his hands against his chest. "Funny sort of pain I've got," thought Johnny. "Wonder if I should shock them if I went in somewhere for a drop of brandy?"

"It don't get any better," reflected Johnny, with some alarm, on reaching the corner of Cheapside. "Hope I'm not going to be ill. Whatever—" The explanation came to him. "Of course, it's these damned stays! No wonder girls are short-tempered, at times."

At the offices of the Marble Soap, Johnny was treated with marked courtesy. Mr. Jowett was out, was not expected back till five o'clock. Would the lady wait, or would she call again? The lady decided, now she was there, to wait. Would the lady take the easy-chair? Would the lady have the window open or would she have it shut? Had the lady seen *The Times*?

"Or the *Ha'penny Joker*?" suggested a junior clerk, who thereupon was promptly sent back to his work.

Many of the senior clerks had occasion to pass through the waiting-room. Two of the senior clerks held views about the weather which they appeared wishful to express at length. Johnny began to enjoy himself. This thing was going to be good fun. By the time the slamming of doors and the hurrying of feet announced the advent of the chief, Johnny was looking forward to his interview.

It was briefer and less satisfactory than he had anticipated. Mr. Jowett was very busy—did not as a rule see anybody in the after-noon; but of course, a lady—"Would Miss—"

"Montgomery."

"Would Miss Montgomery inform Mr. Jowett what it was he might have the pleasure of doing for her?"

Miss Montgomery explained.

Mr. Jowett seemed half angry, half amused.

"Really," said Mr. Jowett, "this is hardly playing the game. Against our fellow-men we can protect ourselves, but if the ladies are going to attack us—really it isn't fair."

Miss Montgomery pleaded.

"I'll think it over," was all that Mr. Jowett could be made to promise. "Look me up again."

"When?" asked Miss Montgomery.

"What's to-day?—Thursday. Say Monday." Mr. Jowett rang the bell. "Take my advice," said the old gentleman, laying a fatherly hand on Johnny's shoulder, "leave business to us men. You are a handsome girl. You can do better for yourself than this."

A clerk entered, Johnny rose.

"On Monday next, then," Johnny reminded him.

"At four o'clock," agreed Mr. Jowett. "Good afternoon."

Johnny went out feeling disappointed, and yet, as he told himself, he hadn't done so badly. Anyhow, there was nothing for it but to wait till Monday. Now he would go home, change his clothes, and get some dinner. He hailed a hansom.

"Number twenty-eight—no. Stop at the Queen's Street corner of Lincoln's Inn Fields," Johnny directed the man.

"Quite right, miss," commented the cabman pleasantly. "Corner's best—saves all talk."

"What do you mean?" demanded Johnny.

"No offence, miss," answered the man. "We was all young once."

Johnny climbed in. At the corner of Queen Street and Lincoln's Inn Fields, Johnny got out. Johnny, who had been pondering other matters, put his hand instinctively to where, speaking generally, his pocket should have been; then recollected himself.

"Let me see, did I think to bring any money out with me, or did I not?" mused Johnny, as he stood upon the kerb.

"Look in the ridicule, miss," suggested the cabman.

Johnny looked. It was empty.

"Perhaps I put it in my pocket," thought Johnny.

The cabman hitched his reins to the whip-socket and leant back.

"It's somewhere about here, I know, I saw it," Johnny told himself. "Sorry to keep you waiting," Johnny added aloud to the cabman.

"Don't you worry about that, miss," replied the cabman civilly; "we are used to it. A shilling a quarter of an hour is what we charge."

"Of all the damned silly tricks!" muttered Johnny to himself.

Two small boys and a girl carrying a baby paused, interested.

"Go away," told them the cabman. "You'll have troubles of your own one day."

The urchins moved a few steps further, then halted again and were joined by a slatternly woman and another boy.

"Got it!" cried Johnny, unable to suppress his delight as his hand slipped through a fold. The lady with the baby, without precisely knowing why, set up a shrill cheer. Johnny's delight died away; it wasn't the pocket-hole. Short of taking the skirt off and turning it inside out, it didn't seem to Johnny that he ever would find that pocket.

Then in that moment of despair he came across it accidentally. It was as empty as the reticule!

"I am sorry," said Johnny to the cabman, "but I appear to have come out without my purse."

The cabman said he had heard that tale before, and was making preparations to descend. The crowd, now numbering eleven, looked hopeful. It occurred to Johnny later that he might have offered his umbrella to the cabman; at least it would have fetched the eighteen-pence. One thinks of these things afterwards. The only idea that occurred to him at the moment was that of getting home.

"'Ere, 'old my 'orse a minute, one of yer," shouted the cabman.

Half a dozen willing hands seized the dozing steed and roused it into madness.

"Hi! stop 'er!" roared the cabman.

"She's down!" shouted the excited crowd.

"Tripped over 'er skirt," explained the slatternly woman. "They do 'amper you."

"No, she's not. She's up again!" vociferated a delighted plumb-er, with a sounding slap on his own leg. "Gor blimy, if she ain't a good 'un!"

Fortunately the Square was tolerably clear and Johnny a good runner. Holding now his skirt and petticoat high in his left hand, Johnny moved across the Square at the rate of fifteen miles an hour. A butcher's boy sprang in front of him with arms held out to stop him. The thing that for the next three months annoyed that butcher boy most was hearing shouted out after him "Yah! who was knocked down and run over by a lidy?" By the time Johnny reached the Strand, *via* Clement's Inn, the hue and cry was far behind. Johnny dropped his skirts and assumed a more girlish pace. Through Bow Street and Long Acre he reached Great Queen Street in safety. Upon his own doorstep he began to laugh. His afternoon's experience had been amusing; still, on the whole, he wasn't sorry it was over. One can have too much even of the best of jokes. Johnny rang the bell.

The door opened. Johnny would have walked in had not a big, raw-boned woman barred his progress.

"What do you want?" demanded the raw-boned woman.

"Want to come in," explained Johnny.

"What do you want to come in for?"

This appeared to Johnny a foolish question. On reflection he saw the sense of it. This raw-boned woman was not Mrs. Pegg, his landlady. Some friend of hers, he supposed.

"It's all right," said Johnny, "I live here. Left my latchkey at home, that's all."

"There's no females lodging here," declared the raw-boned lady. "And what's more, there's going to be none."

All this was very vexing. Johnny, in his joy at reaching his own doorstep, had not foreseen these complications. Now it would be necessary to explain things. He only hoped the story would not get round to the fellows at the club.

"Ask Mrs. Pegg to step up for a minute," requested Johnny.

"Not at 'ome," explained the raw-boned lady.

"Not—not at home?"

"Gone to Romford, if you wish to know, to see her mother."

"Gone to Romford?"

"I said Romford, didn't I?" retorted the raw-boned lady, tartly.

"What—what time do you expect her in?"

"Sunday evening, six o'clock," replied the raw-boned lady.

Johnny looked at the raw-boned lady, imagined himself telling the raw-boned lady the simple, unvarnished truth, and the raw-boned lady's utter disbelief of every word of it. An inspiration came to his aid.

"I am Mr. Bulstrode's sister," said Johnny meekly; "he's expecting me."

"Thought you said you lived here?" reminded him the raw-boned lady.

"I meant that he lived here," replied poor Johnny still more meekly. "He has the second floor, you know."

"I know," replied the raw-boned lady. "Not in just at present."

"Not in?"

"Went out at three o'clock."

"I'll go up to his room and wait for him," said Johnny.

"No, you won't," said the raw-boned lady.

For an instant it occurred to Johnny to make a dash for it, but the raw-boned lady looked both formidable and determined. There would be a big disturbance—perhaps the police called in. Johnny had often wanted to see his name in print: in connection with this affair he somehow felt he didn't.

"Do let me in," Johnny pleaded; "I have nowhere else to go."

"You have a walk and cool yourself," suggested the raw-boned lady. "Don't expect he will be long."

"But, you see—"

The raw-boned lady slammed the door.

Outside a restaurant in Wellington Street, from which proceeded savoury odours, Johnny paused and tried to think.

"What the devil did I do with that umbrella? I had it—no, I didn't. Must have dropped it, I suppose, when that silly ass tried to stop me. By Jove! I am having luck!"

Outside another restaurant in the Strand Johnny paused again. "How am I to live till Sunday night? Where am I to sleep? If I telegraph home—damn it! how can I telegraph? I haven't got a penny. This is funny," said Johnny, unconsciously speaking aloud; "upon my word, this is funny! Oh! you go to—."

Johnny hurled this last at the head of an overgrown errand-boy whose intention had been to offer sympathy.

"Well, I never!" commented a passing flower-girl. "Calls 'erself a lidy, I suppose."

"Nowadays," observed the stud and button merchant at the corner of Exeter Street, "they make 'em out of anything."

Drawn by a notion that was forming in his mind, Johnny turned his steps up Bedford Street. "Why not?" mused Johnny. "Nobody else seems to have a suspicion. Why should they? I'll never hear the last of it if they find me out. But why should they find me out? Well, something's got to be done."

Johnny walked on quickly. At the door of the Autolycus Club he was undecided for a moment, then took his courage in both hands and plunged through the swing doors.

"Is Mr. Herring—Mr. Jack Herring—here?"

"Find him in the smoking-room, Mr. Bulstrode," answered old Goslin, who was reading the evening paper.

"Oh, would you mind asking him to step out a moment?"

Old Goslin looked up, took off his spectacles, rubbed them, put them on again.

"Please say Miss Bulstrode—Mr. Bulstrode's sister."

Old Goslin found Jack Herring the centre of an earnest argument on Hamlet—was he really mad?

"A lady to see you, Mr. Herring," announced old Goslin.

"A what?"

"Miss Bulstrode—Mr. Bulstrode's sister. She's waiting in the hall."

"Never knew he had a sister," said Jack Herring, rising.

"Wait a minute," said Harry Bennett. "Shut that door. Don't go." This to old Goslin, who closed the door and returned. "Lady in a heliotrope dress with a lace collar, three flounces on the skirt?"

"That's right, Mr. Bennett," agreed old Goslin.

"It's the Babe himself!" asserted Harry Bennett.

The question of Hamlet's madness was forgotten.

"Was in at Stinchcombe's this morning," explained Harry Bennett; "saw the clothes on the counter addressed to him. That's the identical frock. This is just a 'try on'—thinks he's going to have a lark with us."

The Autolycus Club looked round at itself.

"I can see verra promising possibilities in this, provided the thing is properly managed," said the Wee Laddie, after a pause.

"So can I," agreed Jack Herring. "Keep where you are, all of you. 'Twould be a pity to fool it."

The Autolycus Club waited. Jack Herring re-entered the room.

"One of the saddest stories I have ever heard in all my life," explained Jack Herring in a whisper. "Poor girl left Derbyshire this morning to come and see her brother; found him out—hasn't been seen at his lodgings since three o'clock; fears something may have happened to him. Landlady gone to Romford to see her mother; strange woman in charge, won't let her in to wait for him."

"How sad it is when trouble overtakes the innocent and helpless!" murmured Somerville the Briefless.

"That's not the worst of it," continued Jack. "The dear girl has been robbed of everything she possesses, even of her umbrella, and hasn't got a *sou*; hasn't had any dinner, and doesn't know where to sleep."

"Sounds a bit elaborate," thought Porson.

"I think I can understand it," said the Briefless one. "What has happened is this. He's dressed up thinking to have a bit of fun with us, and has come out, forgetting to put any money or his latchkey in his pocket. His landlady may have gone to Romford or may not. In any case, he would have to knock at the door and enter into explanations. What does he suggest—the loan of a sovereign?"

"The loan of two," replied Jack Herring.

"To buy himself a suit of clothes. Don't you do it, Jack. Providence has imposed this upon us. Our duty is to show him the folly of indulging in senseless escapades."

"I think we might give him a dinner," thought the stout and sympathetic Porson.

"What I propose to do," grinned Jack, "is to take him round to Mrs. Postwhistle's. She's under a sort of obligation to me. It was I who got her the post office. We'll leave him there for a night, with instructions to Mrs. P. to keep a motherly eye on him. To-morrow he shall have his 'bit of fun,' and I guess he'll be the first to get tired of the joke."

It looked a promising plot. Seven members of the Autolycus Club gallantly undertook to accompany "Miss Bulstrode" to her lodgings. Jack Herring excited jealousy by securing the privilege of carrying her reticule. "Miss Bulstrode" was given to understand that anything any of the seven could do for her, each and every would be delighted to do, if only for the sake of her brother, one of the dearest boys that ever breathed—a bit of an ass, though that, of course, he could not help. "Miss Bulstrode" was not as grateful as perhaps she should have been. Her idea still was that if one of them would lend her a couple of sovereigns, the rest need not worry themselves further. This, purely in her own interests, they declined to do. She had suffered one extensive robbery that day already, as Jack reminded her. London was a city of danger to the young and inexperienced. Far better that they should watch over her and provide for her simple wants. Painful as it was to refuse a lady, a beloved companion's sister's welfare was yet dearer to them. "Miss Bulstrode's" only desire was not to waste their time. Jack Herring's opinion was that there existed no true Englishman who would grudge time spent upon succouring a beautiful maiden in distress.

Arrived at the little grocer's shop in Rolls Court, Jack Herring drew Mrs. Postwhistle aside.

"She's the sister of a very dear friend of ours," explained Jack Herring.

"A fine-looking girl," commented Mrs. Postwhistle.

"I shall be round again in the morning. Don't let her out of your sight, and, above all, don't lend her any money," directed Jack Herring.

"I understand," replied Mrs. Postwhistle.

"Miss Bulstrode" having despatched an excellent supper of cold mutton and bottled beer, leant back in her chair and crossed her legs.

"I have often wondered," remarked Miss Bulstrode, her eyes fixed upon the ceiling, "what a cigarette would taste like."

"Taste nasty, I should say, the first time," thought Mrs. Postwhistle, who was knitting.

"Some girls, so I have heard," remarked Miss Bulstrode, "smoke cigarettes."

"Not nice girls," thought Mrs. Postwhistle.

"One of the nicest girls I ever knew," remarked Miss Bulstrode, "always smoked a cigarette after supper. Said it soothed her nerves."

"Wouldn't 'ave thought so if I'd 'ad charge of 'er," said Mrs. Postwhistle.

"I think," said Miss Bulstrode, who seemed restless, "I think I shall go for a little walk before turning in."

"Perhaps it would do us good," agreed Mrs. Postwhistle, laying down her knitting.

"Don't you trouble to come," urged the thoughtful Miss Bulstrode. "You look tired."

"Not at all," replied Mrs. Postwhistle. "Feel I should like it."

In some respects Mrs. Postwhistle proved an admirable companion. She asked no questions, and only spoke when spoken to, which, during that walk, was not often. At the end of half an hour, Miss Bulstrode pleaded a headache and thought she would return home and go to bed. Mrs. Postwhistle thought it a reasonable idea.

"Well, it's better than tramping the streets," muttered Johnny, as the bedroom door was closed behind him, "and that's all one can say for it. Must get hold of a smoke to-morrow, if I have to rob the till. What's that?" Johnny stole across on, tiptoe. "Confound it!" said Johnny, "if she hasn't locked the door!"

Johnny sat down upon the bed and took stock of his position. "It doesn't seem to me," thought Johnny, "that I'm ever going to get out of this mess." Johnny, still muttering, unfastened his stays. "Thank

God, that's off!" ejaculated Johnny piously, as he watched his form slowly expanding. "Suppose I'll be used to them before I've finished with them."

Johnny had a night of dreams.

For the whole of next day, which was Friday, Johnny remained "Miss Bulstrode," hoping against hope to find an opportunity to escape from his predicament without confession. The entire Autolycus Club appeared to have fallen in love with him.

"Thought I was a bit of a fool myself," mused Johnny, "where a petticoat was concerned. Don't believe these blithering idiots have ever seen a girl before."

They came in ones, they came in little parties, and tendered him devotion. Even Mrs. Postwhistle, accustomed to regard human phenomena without comment, remarked upon it.

"When you are all tired of it," said Mrs. Postwhistle to Jack Herring, "let me know."

"The moment we find her brother," explained Jack Herring, "of course we shall take her to him."

"Nothing like looking in the right place for a thing when you've finished looking in the others," observed Mrs. Postwhistle.

"What do you mean?" demanded Jack.

"Just what I say," answered Mrs. Postwhistle.

Jack Herring looked at Mrs. Postwhistle. But Mrs. Postwhistle's face was not of the expressive order.

"Post office still going strong?" asked Jack Herring.

"The post office 'as been a great 'elp to me," admitted Mrs. Postwhistle; "and I'm not forgetting that I owe it to you."

"Don't mention it," murmured Jack Herring.

They brought her presents—nothing very expensive, more as tokens of regard: dainty packets of sweets, nosegays of simple flowers, bottles of scent. To Somerville "Miss Bulstrode" hinted that if he really did desire to please her, and wasn't merely talking through his hat—Miss Bulstrode apologised for the slang, which, she feared, she must have picked up from her brother—he might give her a box of Messani's cigarettes, size No. 2. The suggestion pained him. Somerville the Briefless was perhaps old-fashioned. Miss Bulstrode cut him short by agreeing that he was, and seemed disinclined for further conversation.

They took her to Madame Tussaud's. They took her up the Monument. They took her to the Tower of London. In the evening they took her to the Polytechnic to see Pepper's Ghost. They made a merry party wherever they went.

"Seem to be enjoying themselves!" remarked other sightseers, surprised and envious.

"Girl seems to be a bit out of it," remarked others, more observant.

"Sulky-looking bit o' goods, I call her," remarked some of the ladies.

The fortitude with which Miss Bulstrode bore the mysterious disappearance of her brother excited admiration.

"Hadn't we better telegraph to your people in Derbyshire?" suggested Jack Herring.

"Don't do it," vehemently protested the thoughtful Miss Bulstrode; "it might alarm them. The best plan is for you to lend me a couple of sovereigns and let me return home quietly."

"You might be robbed again," feared Jack Herring. "I'll go down with you."

"Perhaps he'll turn up to-morrow," thought Miss Bulstrode. "Expect he's gone on a visit."

"He ought not to have done it," thought Jack Herring, "knowing you were coming."

"Oh! he's like that," explained Miss Bulstrode.

"If I had a young and beautiful sister—" said Jack Herring.

"Oh! let's talk of something else," suggested Miss Bulstrode. "You make me tired."

With Jack Herring, in particular, Johnny was beginning to lose patience. That "Miss Bulstrode's" charms had evidently struck Jack Herring all of a heap, as the saying is, had in the beginning amused Master Johnny. Indeed—as in the seclusion of his bedchamber over the little grocer's shop he told himself with bitter self-reproach—he had undoubtedly encouraged the man. From admiration Jack had rapidly passed to infatuation, from infatuation to apparent imbecility. Had Johnny's mind been less intent upon his own troubles, he might have been suspicious. As it was, and after all that had happened, nothing now could astonish Johnny. "Thank Heaven," murmured Johnny, as he blew out the light, "this Mrs. Postwhistle appears to be a reliable woman."

Now, about the same time that Johnny's head was falling thus upon his pillow, the Autolycus Club sat discussing plans for their next day's entertainment.

"I think," said Jack Herring, "the Crystal Palace in the morning when it's nice and quiet."

"To be followed by Greenwich Hospital in the afternoon," suggested Somerville.

"Winding up with the Moore and Burgess Minstrels in the evening," thought Porson.

"Hardly the place for the young person," feared Jack Herring. "Some of the jokes—"

"Mr. Brandram gives a reading of *Julius Caesar* at St. George's Hall," the Wee Laddie informed them for their guidance.

"Hallo!" said Alexander the Poet, entering at the moment. "What are you all talking about?"

"We were discussing where to take Miss Bulstrode to-morrow evening," informed him Jack Herring.

"Miss Bulstrode," repeated the Poet in a tone of some surprise. "Do you mean Johnny Bulstrode's sister?"

"That's the lady," answered Jack. "But how do you come to know about her? Thought you were in Yorkshire."

"Came up yesterday," explained the Poet. "Travelled up with her."

"Travelled up with her?"

"From Matlock Bath. What's the matter with you all?" demanded the Poet. "You all of you look—"

"Sit down," said the Briefless one to the Poet. "Let's talk this matter over quietly."

Alexander the Poet, mystified, sat down.

"You say you travelled up to London yesterday with Miss Bulstrode. You are sure it was Miss Bulstrode?"

"Sure!" retorted the Poet. "Why, I've known her ever since she was a baby."

"About what time did you reach London?"

"Three-thirty."

"And what became of her? Where did she say she was going?"

"I never asked her. The last I saw of her she was getting into a cab. I had an appointment myself, and was—I say, what's the matter with Herring?"

Herring had risen and was walking about with his head between his hands.

"Never mind him. Miss Bulstrode is a lady of about—how old?"

"Eighteen—no, nineteen last birthday."

"A tall, handsome sort of girl?"

"Yes. I say, has anything happened to her?"

"Nothing has happened to her," assured him Somerville. "*She's all right. Been having rather a good time, on the whole.*"

The Poet was relieved to hear it.

"I asked her an hour ago," said Jack Herring, who was still holding his head between his hands as if to make sure it was there, "if she thought she could ever learn to love me. Would you say that could be construed into an offer of marriage?"

The remainder of the Club was unanimously of opinion that, practically speaking, it was a proposal.

"I don't see it," argued Jack Herring. "It was merely in the nature of a remark."

The Club was of opinion that such quibbling was unworthy of a gentleman.

It appeared to be a case for prompt action. Jack Herring sat down and then and there began a letter to Miss Bulstrode, care of Mrs. Postwhistle.

"But what I don't understand—" said Alexander the Poet.

"Oh! take him away somewhere and tell him, someone," moaned Jack Herring. "How can I think with all this chatter going on?"

"But why did Bennett—" whispered Porson.

"Where is Bennett?" demanded half a dozen fierce voices.

Harry Bennett had not been seen all day.

Jack's letter was delivered to "Miss Bulstrode" the next morning at breakfast-time. Having perused it, Miss Bulstrode rose and requested of Mrs. Postwhistle the loan of half a crown.

"Mr. Herring's particular instructions were," explained Mrs. Postwhistle, "that, above all things, I was not to lend you any money."

"When you have read that," replied Miss Bulstrode, handing her the letter, "perhaps you will agree with me that Herring is—an ass."

Mrs. Postwhistle read the letter and produced the half-crown.

"Better get a shave with part of it," suggested Mrs. Postwhistle. "That is, if you are going to play the fool much longer."

"Miss Bulstrode" opened his eyes. Mrs. Postwhistle went on with her breakfast.

"Don't tell them," said Johnny; "not just for a little while, at all events."

"Nothing to do with me," replied Mrs. Postwhistle.

Twenty minutes later, the real Miss Bulstrode, on a visit to her aunt in Kensington, was surprised at receiving, enclosed in an envelope, the following hastily scrawled note:—

"Want to speak to you at once—alone. Don't yell when you see me. It's all right. Can explain in two ticks.—Your loving brother,

JOHNNY."

It took longer than two ticks; but at last the Babe came to an end of it.

"When you have done laughing," said the Babe.

"But you look so ridiculous," said his sister.

"*They* didn't think so," retorted the Babe. "I took them in all right. Guess you've never had as much attention, all in one day."

"Are you sure you took them in?" queried his sister.

"If you will come to the Club at eight o'clock this evening," said the Babe, "I'll prove it to you. Perhaps I'll take you on to a theatre afterwards—if you're good."

The Babe himself walked into the Autolycus Club a few minutes before eight and encountered an atmosphere of restraint.

"Thought you were lost," remarked Somerville coldly.

"Called away suddenly—very important business," explained the Babe. "Awfully much obliged to all you fellows for all you have been doing for my sister. She's just been telling me."

"Don't mention it," said two or three.

"Awfully good of you, I'm sure," persisted the Babe. "Don't know what she would have done without you."

A mere nothing, the Club assured him. The blushing modesty of the Autolycus Club at hearing of their own good deeds was touching. Left to themselves, they would have talked of quite other things. As a matter of fact, they tried to.

"Never heard her speak so enthusiastically of anyone as she does of you, Jack," said the Babe, turning to Jack Herring.

"Of course, you know, dear boy," explained Jack Herring, "anything I could do for a sister of yours—"

"I know, dear boy," replied the Babe; "I always felt it."

"Say no more about it," urged Jack Herring.

"She couldn't quite make out that letter of yours this morning," continued the Babe, ignoring Jack's request. "She's afraid you think her ungrateful."

"It seemed to me, on reflection," explained Jack Herring, "that on one or two little matters she may have misunderstood me. As I wrote her, there are days when I don't seem altogether to quite know what I'm doing."

"Rather awkward," thought the Babe.

"It is," agreed Jack Herring. "Yesterday was one of them."

"She tells me you were most kind to her," the Babe reassured him. "She thought at first it was a little uncivil, your refusing to lend her any money. But as I put it to her—"

"It was silly of me," interrupted Jack. "I see that now. I went round this morning meaning to make it all right. But she was gone, and Mrs. Postwhistle seemed to think I had better leave things as they were. I blame myself exceedingly."

"My dear boy, don't blame yourself for anything. You acted nobly," the Babe told him. "She's coming here to call for me this evening on purpose to thank you."

"I'd rather not," said Jack Herring.

"Nonsense," said the Babe.

"You must excuse me," insisted Jack Herring. "I don't mean it rudely, but really I'd rather not see her."

"But here she is," said the Babe, taking at that moment the card from old Goslin's hand. "She will think it so strange."

"I'd really rather not," repeated poor Jack.

"It seems discourteous," suggested Somerville.

"You go," suggested Jack.

"She doesn't want to see me," explained Somerville.

"Yes she does," corrected him the Babe.

"I'd forgotten, she wants to see you both."

"If I go," said Jack, "I shall tell her the plain truth."

"Do you know," said Somerville, "I'm thinking that will be the shortest way."

Miss Bulstrode was seated in the hall. Jack Herring and Somerville both thought her present quieter style of dress suited her much better.

"Here he is," announced the Babe, in triumph. "Here's Jack Herring and here's Somerville. Do you know, I could hardly persuade them to come out and see you. Dear old Jack, he always was so shy."

Miss Bulstrode rose. She said she could never thank them sufficiently for all their goodness to her. Miss Bulstrode seemed quite overcome. Her voice trembled with emotion.

"Before we go further, Miss Bulstrode," said Jack Herring, "it will be best to tell you that all along we thought you were your brother, dressed up as a girl."

"Oh!" said the Babe, "so that's the explanation, is it? If I had only known—" Then the Babe stopped, and wished he hadn't spoken.

Somerville seized him by the shoulders and, with a sudden jerk, stood him beside his sister under the gas-jet.

"You little brute!" said Somerville. "It was you all along." And the Babe, seeing the game was up, and glad that the joke had not been entirely on one side, confessed.

Jack Herring and Somerville the Briefless went that night with Johnny and his sister to the theatre—and on other nights. Miss Bulstrode thought Jack Herring very nice, and told her brother so. But she thought Somerville the Briefless even nicer, and later, under cross-examination, when Somerville was no longer briefless, told Somerville so himself.

But that has nothing to do with this particular story, the end of which is that Miss Bulstrode kept the appointment made for Monday afternoon between "Miss Montgomery" and Mr. Jowett, and secured thereby the Marble Soap advertisement for the back page of *Good Humour* for six months, at twenty-five pounds a week.

STORY THE SEVENTH

Dick Danvers Presents His Petition

ILLIAM CLODD, mopping his brow, laid down the screwdriver, and stepping back, regarded the result of his labours with evident satisfaction.

"It looks like a bookcase," said William Clodd. "You might sit in the room for half an hour and never know it wasn't a bookcase."

What William Clodd had accomplished was this: he had had prepared, after his own design, what appeared to be four shelves laden with works suggestive of thought and erudition. As a matter of fact, it was not a bookcase, but merely a flat board, the books merely the backs of volumes that had long since found their way into the paper-mill. This artful deception William Clodd had screwed upon a cottage piano standing in the corner of the editorial office of *Good Humour*. Half a dozen real volumes piled upon the top of the piano completed the illusion. As William Clodd had proudly remarked, a casual visitor might easily have been deceived.

"If you had to sit in the room while she was practising mixed scales, you'd be quickly undeceived," said the editor of *Good Humour*, one Peter Hope. He spoke bitterly.

"You are not always in," explained Clodd. "There must be hours when she is here alone, with nothing else to do. Besides, you will get used to it after a while."

"You, I notice, don't try to get used to it," snarled Peter Hope. "You always go out the moment she commences."

"A friend of mine," continued William Clodd, "worked in an office over a piano-shop for seven years, and when the shop closed, it nearly ruined his business; couldn't settle down to work for want of it."

"Why doesn't he come here?" asked Peter Hope. "The floor above is vacant."

"Can't," explained William Clodd. "He's dead."

"I can quite believe it," commented Peter Hope.

"It was a shop where people came and practised, paying sixpence an hour, and he had got to like it—said it made a cheerful background to his thoughts. Wonderful what you can get accustomed to."

"What's the good of it?" demanded Peter Hope.

"What's the good of it!" retorted William Clodd indignantly. "Every girl ought to know how to play the piano. A nice thing if when her lover asks her to play something to him—"

"I wonder you don't start a matrimonial agency," sneered Peter Hope. "Love and marriage—you think of nothing else."

"When you are bringing up a young girl—" argued Clodd.

"But you're not," interrupted Peter; "that's just what I'm trying to get out of your head. It is I who am bringing her up. And between ourselves, I wish you wouldn't interfere so much."

"You are not fit to bring up a girl."

"I've brought her up for seven years without your help. She's my adopted daughter, not yours. I do wish people would learn to mind their own business."

"You've done very well—"

"Thank you," said Peter Hope sarcastically. "It's very kind of you. Perhaps when you've time, you'll write me out a testimonial."

"—up till now," concluded the imperturbable Clodd. "A girl of eighteen wants to know something else besides mathematics and the classics. You don't understand them."

"I do understand them," asserted Peter Hope. "What do you know about them? You're not a father."

"You've done your best," admitted William Clodd in a tone of patronage that irritated Peter greatly; "but you're a dreamer; you don't know the world. The time is coming when the girl will have to think of a husband."

"There's no need for her to think of a husband, not for years," retorted Peter Hope. "And even when she does, is strumming on the piano going to help her?"

"I tink—I tink," said Dr. Smith, who had hitherto remained a silent listener, "our young frent Clodd is right. You haf never quite got over your idea dat she was going to be a boy. You haf taught her de tings a boy should know."

"You cut her hair," added Clodd.

"I don't," snapped Peter.

"You let her have it cut—it's the same thing. At eighteen she knows more about the ancient Greeks and Romans than she does about her own frocks."

"De young girl," argued the doctor, "what is she? De flower dat makes bright for us de garden of life, de gurgling brook dat murmurs by de dusty highway, de cheerful fire—"

"She can't be all of them," snapped Peter, who was a stickler for style. "Do keep to one simile at a time."

"Now you listen to plain sense," said William Clodd. "You want—we all want—the girl to be a success all round."

"I want her—" Peter Hope was rummaging among the litter on the desk. It certainly was not there. Peter pulled out a drawer-two drawers. "I wish," said Peter Hope, "I wish sometimes she wasn't quite so clever."

The old doctor rummaged among dusty files of papers in a corner. Clodd found it on the mantelpiece concealed beneath the hollow foot of a big brass candlestick, and handed it to Peter.

Peter had one vice—the taking in increasing quantities of snuff, which was harmful for him, as he himself admitted. Tommy, sympathetic to most masculine frailties, was severe, however, upon this one.

"You spill it upon your shirt and on your coat," had argued Tommy. "I like to see you always neat. Besides, it isn't a nice habit. I do wish, dad, you'd give it up."

"I must," Peter had agreed. "I'll break myself of it. But not all at once—it would be a wrench; by degrees, Tommy, by degrees."

So a compromise had been compounded. Tommy was to hide the snuff-box. It was to be somewhere in the room and to be accessible, but that was all. Peter, when self-control had reached the breaking-point, might try and find it. Occasionally, luck helping Peter, he would find it early in the day, when he would earn his own bitter self-reproaches by indulging in quite an orgie. But more often Tommy's artfulness was such that he would be compelled, by want of time, to abandon the search. Tommy always knew when he had failed by the air of indignant resignation with which he would greet her on her return. Then perhaps towards evening, Peter, looking up, would see the box open before his nose, above it, a pair of reproving black eyes, their severity counterbalanced by a pair of full red lips trying not to smile. And Peter, knowing that only one pinch would be permitted, would dip deeply.

"I want her," said Peter Hope, feeling with his snuff-box in his hand more confidence in his own judgment, "to be a sensible, clever woman, capable of earning her own living and of being independent; not a mere helpless doll, crying for some man to come and take care of her."

"A woman's business," asserted Clodd, "is to be taken care of."

"Some women, perhaps," admitted Peter; "but Tommy, you know very well, is not going to be the ordinary type of woman. She has brains; she will make her way in the world."

"It doesn't depend upon brains," said Clodd. "She hasn't got the elbows."

"The elbows?"

"They are not sharp enough. The last 'bus home on a wet night tells you whether a woman is capable of pushing her own way in the world. Tommy's the sort to get left on the kerb."

"She's the sort," retorted Peter, "to make a name for herself and to be able to afford a cab. Don't you bully me!" Peter sniffed self-assertiveness from between his thumb and finger.

"Yes, I shall," Clodd told him, "on this particular point. The poor girl's got no mother."

Fortunately for the general harmony the door opened at the moment to admit the subject of discussion.

"Got that *Daisy Blossom* advertisement out of old Blatchley," announced Tommy, waving triumphantly a piece of paper over her head.

"No!" exclaimed Peter. "How did you manage it?"

"Asked him for it," was Tommy's explanation.

"Very odd," mused Peter; "asked the old idiot for it myself only last week. He refused it point-blank."

Clodd snorted reproof. "You know I don't like your doing that sort of thing. It isn't proper for a young girl—"

"It's all right," assured him Tommy; "he's bald!"

"That makes no difference," was Clodd's opinion.

"Yes it does," was Tommy's. "I like them bald."

Tommy took Peter's head between her hands and kissed it, and in doing so noticed the tell-tale specks of snuff.

"Just a pinch, my dear," explained Peter, "the merest pinch."

Tommy took up the snuff-box from the desk. "I'll show you where I'm going to put it this time." She put it in her pocket. Peter's face fell.

"What do you think of it?" said Clodd. He led her to the corner. "Good idea, ain't it?"

"Why, where's the piano?" demanded Tommy.

Clodd turned in delighted triumph to the others.

"Humbug!" growled Peter.

"It isn't humbug," cried Clodd indignantly. "She thought it was a bookcase—anybody would. You'll be able to sit there and practise by the hour," explained Clodd to Tommy. "When you hear anybody coming up the stairs, you can leave off."

"How can she hear anything when she—" A bright idea occurred to Peter. "Don't you think, Clodd, as a practical man," suggested Peter insinuatingly, adopting the Socratic method, "that if we got her one of those dummy pianos—you know what I mean; it's just like an ordinary piano, only you don't hear it?"

Clodd shook his head. "No good at all. Can't tell the effect she is producing."

"Quite so. Then, on the other hand, Clodd, don't you think that hearing the effect they are producing may sometimes discourage the beginner?"

Clodd's opinion was that such discouragement was a thing to be battled with.

Tommy, who had seated herself, commenced a scale in contrary motion.

"Well, I'm going across to the printer's now," explained Clodd, taking up his hat. "Got an appointment with young Grindley at three. You stick to it. A spare half-hour now and then that you never miss does wonders. You've got it in you." With these encouraging remarks to Tommy, Clodd disappeared.

"Easy for him," muttered Peter bitterly. "Always does have an appointment outside the moment she begins."

Tommy appeared to be throwing her very soul into the performance. Passers-by in Crane Court paused, regarded the first-floor windows of the publishing and editorial offices of *Good Humour* with troubled looks, then hurried on.

"She has—remarkably firm douch!" shouted the doctor into Peter's ear. "Will see you—evening. Someting—say to you."

The fat little doctor took his hat and departed. Tommy, ceasing suddenly, came over and seated herself on the arm of Peter's chair.

"Feeling grumpy?" asked Tommy.

"It isn't," explained Peter, "that I mind the noise. I'd put up with that if I could see the good of it."

"It's going to help me to get a husband, dad. Seems to me an odd way of doing it; but Billy says so, and Billy knows all about everything."

"I can't understand you, a sensible girl, listening to such nonsense," said Peter. "It's that that troubles me."

"Dad, where are your wits?" demanded Tommy. "Isn't Billy acting like a brick? Why, he could go into Fleet Street to half a dozen other papers and make five hundred a year as advertising-agent—you know he could. But he doesn't. He sticks to us. If my making myself ridiculous with that tin pot they persuaded him was a piano is going to please him, isn't it common sense and sound business, to say nothing of good nature and gratitude, for me to do it? Dad, I've got a surprise for him. Listen." And Tommy, springing from the arm of Peter's chair, returned to the piano.

"What was it?" questioned Tommy, having finished. "Could you recognise it?"

"I think," said Peter, "it sounded like—It wasn't 'Home, Sweet Home,' was it?"

Tommy clapped her hands. "Yes, it was. You'll end by liking it yourself, dad. We'll have musical 'At Homes.'"

"Tommy, have I brought you up properly, do you think?"

"No dad, you haven't. You have let me have my own way too much. You know the proverb: 'Good mothers make bad daughters.' Clodd's right; you've spoilt me, dad. Do you remember, dad, when I first came to you, seven years ago, a ragged little brat out of the streets, that didn't know itself whether 'twas a boy or a girl? Do you know what I thought to myself the moment I set eyes on you? 'Here's a soft old juggins; I'll be all right if I can get in here!' It makes you smart, knocking about in the gutters and being knocked about; you read faces quickly."

"Do you remember your cooking, Tommy? You 'had an aptitude for it,' according to your own idea."

Tommy laughed. "I wonder how you stood it."

"You were so obstinate. You came to me as 'cook and housekeeper,' and as cook and housekeeper, and as nothing else, would you remain. If I suggested any change, up would go your chin into the air. I dared not even dine out too often, you were such a little tyrant. The only thing you were always ready to do, if I wasn't satisfied, was to march out of the house and leave me. Wherever did you get that savage independence of yours?"

"I don't know. I think it must have been from a woman—perhaps she was my mother; I don't know—who used to sit up in the bed and cough, all night it seemed to me. People would come to see us—ladies in fine clothes, and gentlemen with oily hair. I think they wanted to help us. Many of them had kind voices. But always a hard look would come into her face, and she would tell them what even then I knew to be untrue—it was one of the first things I can recollect—that we had everything we wanted, that we needed no help from anyone. They would go away, shrugging their shoulders. I grew up with the feeling that seemed to have been burnt into my brain, that to take from anybody anything you had not earned was shameful. I don't think I could do it even now, not even from you. I am useful to you, dad—I do help you?"

There had crept a terror into Tommy's voice. Peter felt the little hands upon his arm trembling.

"Help me? Why, you work like a nigger—like a nigger is supposed to work, but doesn't. No one—whatever we paid him—would do half as much. I don't want to make your head more swollen than it is, young woman, but you have talent; I am not sure it is not genius." Peter felt the little hands tighten upon his arm.

"I do want this paper to be a success; that is why I strum upon the piano to please Clodd. Is it humbug?"

"I am afraid it is; but humbug is the sweet oil that helps this whirling world of ours to spin round smoothly. Too much of it cloys: we drop it very gently."

"But you are sure it is only humbug, Tommy?" It was Peter's voice into which fear had entered now. "It is not that you think he understands you better than I do—would do more for you?"

"You want me to tell you all I think of you, and that isn't good for

133

you, dad—not too often. It would be you who would have swelled head then."

"I am jealous, Tommy, jealous of everyone that comes near you. Life is a tragedy for us old folks. We know there must come a day when you will leave the nest, leave us voiceless, ridiculous, flitting among bare branches. You will understand later, when you have children of your own. This foolish talk about a husband! It is worse for a man than it is for the woman. The mother lives again in her child: the man is robbed of all."

"Dad, do you know how old I am?—that you are talking terrible nonsense?"

"He will come, little girl."

"Yes," answered Tommy, "I suppose he will; but not for a long while—oh, not for a very long while. Don't. It frightens me."

"You? Why should it frighten you?"

"The pain. It makes me feel a coward. I want it to come; I want to taste life, to drain the whole cup, to understand, to feel. But that is the boy in me. I am more than half a boy, I always have been. But the woman in me: it shrinks from the ordeal."

"You talk, Tommy, as if love were something terrible."

"There are all things in it; I feel it, dad. It is life in a single draught. It frightens me."

The child was standing with her face hidden behind her hands. Old Peter, always very bad at lying, stood silent, not knowing what consolation to concoct. The shadow passed, and Tommy's laughing eyes looked out again.

"Haven't you anything to do, dad—outside, I mean?"

"You want to get rid of me?"

"Well, I've nothing else to occupy me till the proofs come in. I'm going to practise, hard."

"I think I'll turn over my article on the Embankment," said Peter.

"There's one thing you all of you ought to be grateful to me for," laughed Tommy, as she seated herself at the piano. "I do induce you all to take more fresh air than otherwise you would."

Tommy, left alone, set herself to her task with the energy and thoroughness that were characteristic of her. Struggling with complicated scales, Tommy bent her eyes closer and closer over the pages of *Czerny's Exercises*. Glancing up to turn a page, Tommy, to her surprise, met the eyes of a stranger. They were brown eyes, their expression sympathetic. Below them, looking golden with the sunlight falling on it, was a moustache and beard cut short in Vandyke fashion, not altogether hiding a pleasant mouth, about the corners of which lurked a smile.

"I beg your pardon," said the stranger. "I knocked three times. Perhaps you did not hear me?"

"No, I didn't," confessed Tommy, closing the book of *Czerny's Exercises*, and rising with chin at an angle that, to anyone acquainted with the chart of Tommy's temperament, might have suggested the advisability of seeking shelter.

"This is the editorial office of *Good Humour*, is it not?" inquired the stranger.

"It is."

"Is the editor in?"

"The editor is out."

"The sub-editor?" suggested the stranger.

"I am the sub-editor."

The stranger raised his eyebrows. Tommy, on the contrary, lowered hers.

"Would you mind glancing through that?" The stranger drew from his pocket a folded manuscript. "It will not take you a moment. I ought, of course, to have sent it through the post; but I am so tired of sending things through the post."

The stranger's manner was compounded of dignified impudence combined with pathetic humility. His eyes both challenged and pleaded. Tommy held out her hand for the paper and retired with it behind the protection of the big editorial desk that, flanked on one side by a screen and on the other by a formidable revolving bookcase, stretched fortress-like across the narrow room. The stranger remained standing.

"Yes. It's pretty," criticised the sub-editor. "Worth printing, perhaps, not worth paying for."

"Not merely a—a nominal sum, sufficient to distinguish it from the work of the amateur?"

Tommy pursed her lips. "Poetry is quite a drug in the market. We can get as much as we want of it for nothing."

"Say half a crown," suggested the stranger.

Tommy shot a swift glance across the desk, and for the first time saw the whole of him. He was clad in a threadbare, long, brown ulster—long, that is, it would have been upon an ordinary man, but the stranger happening to be remarkably tall, it appeared on him ridiculously short, reaching only to his knees. Round his neck and tucked into his waistcoat, thus completely hiding the shirt and collar he may have been wearing or may not, was carefully arranged a blue silk muffler. His hands, which were bare, looked blue and cold. Yet the black frock-coat and waistcoat and French grey trousers bore the unmistakable cut of a first-class tailor and fitted him to perfection. His hat, which he had rested on the desk, shone resplendent, and the handle of his silk umbrella was an eagle's head in gold, with two small rubies for the eyes.

"You can leave it if you like," consented Tommy. "I'll speak to the editor about it when he returns."

"You won't forget it?" urged the stranger.

"No," answered Tommy. "I shall not forget it."

Her black eyes were fixed upon the stranger without her being aware of it. She had dropped unconsciously into her "stocktaking" attitude.

"Thank you very much," said the stranger. "I will call again to-morrow."

The stranger, moving backward to the door, went out.

Tommy sat with her face between her hands. *Czerny's Exercises* lay neglected.

"Anybody called?" asked Peter Hope.

"No," answered Tommy. "Oh, just a man. Left this—not bad."

"The old story," mused Peter, as he unfolded the manuscript. "We all of us begin with poetry. Then we take to prose romances; poetry doesn't pay. Finally, we write articles: 'How to be Happy though Married,' 'What shall we do with our Daughters?' It is life summarised. What is it all about?"

"Oh, the usual sort of thing," explained Tommy. "He wants half a crown for it."

"Poor devil! Let him have it."

"That's not business," growled Tommy.

"Nobody will ever know," said Peter. "We'll enter it as 'telegrams.'"

The stranger called early the next day, pocketed his half-crown, and left another manuscript—an essay. Also he left behind him his gold-handled umbrella, taking away with him instead an old alpaca thing Clodd kept in reserve for exceptionally dirty weather. Peter pronounced the essay usable.

"He has a style," said Peter; "he writes with distinction. Make an appointment for me with him."

Clodd, on missing his umbrella, was indignant.

"What's the good of this thing to me?" commented Clodd. "Sort of thing for a dude in a pantomime! The fellow must be a blithering ass!"

Tommy gave to the stranger messages from both when next he called. He appeared more grieved than surprised concerning the umbrellas.

"You don't think Mr. Clodd would like to keep this umbrella in exchange for his own?" he suggested.

"Hardly his style," explained Tommy.

"It's very peculiar," said the stranger, with a smile. "I have been trying to get rid of this umbrella for the last three weeks. Once upon a time, when I preferred to keep my own umbrella, people used to take it by mistake, leaving all kinds of shabby things behind them in exchange. Now, when I'd really like to get quit of it, nobody will have it."

"Why do you want to get rid of it?" asked Tommy. "It looks a very good umbrella."

"You don't know how it hampers me," said the stranger. "I have to live up to it. It requires a certain amount of resolution to enter a cheap restaurant accompanied by that umbrella. When I do, the waiters draw my attention to the most expensive dishes and recommend me special brands of their so-called champagne. They seem quite surprised if I only want a chop and a glass of beer. I haven't always got the courage to disappoint them. It is really becoming quite a curse to me. If I use it to stop a 'bus, three or four hansoms dash up and quarrel over me. I can't do anything I want to do. I want to live simply and inexpensively: it will not let me."

Tommy laughed. "Can't you lose it?"

The stranger laughed also. "Lose it! You have no idea how honest people are. I hadn't myself. The whole world has gone up in my estimation within the last few weeks. People run after me for quite long distances and force it into my hand—people on rainy days who haven't got umbrellas of their own. It is the same with this hat." The stranger sighed as he took it up. "I am always trying to get *off* with something reasonably shabby in exchange for it. I am always found out and stopped."

"Why don't you pawn them?" suggested the practicable Tommy.

The stranger regarded her with admiration.

"Do you know, I never thought of that," said the stranger. "Of course. What a good idea! Thank you so much."

The stranger departed, evidently much relieved.

"Silly fellow," mused Tommy. "They won't give him a quarter of the value, and he will say: 'Thank you so much,' and be quite contented." It worried Tommy a good deal that day, the thought of that stranger's helplessness.

The stranger's name was Richard Danvers. He lived the other side of Holborn, in Featherstone Buildings, but much of his time came to be spent in the offices of *Good Humour*.

Peter liked him. "Full of promise," was Peter's opinion. "His criticism of that article of mine on 'The Education of Woman' showed both sense and feeling. A scholar and a thinker."

Flipp, the office-boy (spelt Philip), liked him; and Flipp's attitude, in general, was censorial. "He's all right," pronounced Flipp; "nothing stuck-up about him. He's got plenty of sense, lying hidden away."

Miss Ramsbotham liked him. "The men—the men we think about at all," explained Miss Ramsbotham—"may be divided into two classes: the men we ought to like, but don't; and the men there is no particular reason for our liking, but that we do. Personally I could get very fond of your friend Dick. There is nothing whatever attractive about him except himself."

Even Tommy liked him in her way, though at times she was severe with him.

"If you mean a big street," grumbled Tommy, who was going over proofs, "why not say a big street? Why must you always call it a 'main artery'?"

"I am sorry," apologised Danvers. "It is not my own idea. You told me to study the higher-class journals."

"I didn't tell you to select and follow all their faults. Here it is again. Your crowd is always a 'hydra-headed monster'; your tea 'the cup that cheers but not inebriates.'"

"I am afraid I am a deal of trouble to you," suggested the staff.

"I am afraid you are," agreed the sub-editor.

"Don't give me up," pleaded the staff. "I misunderstood you, that is all. I will write English for the future."

"Shall be glad if you will," growled the sub-editor.

Dick Danvers rose. "I am so anxious not to get what you call 'the sack' from here."

The sub-editor, mollified, thought the staff need be under no apprehension, provided it showed itself teachable.

"I have been rather a worthless fellow, Miss Hope," confessed Dick Danvers. "I was beginning to despair of myself till I came across you and your father. The atmosphere here—I don't mean the material atmosphere of Crane Court—is so invigorating: its simplicity, its sincerity. I used to have ideals. I tried to stifle them. There is a set that sneers at all that sort of thing. Now I see that they are good. You will help me?"

Every woman is a mother. Tommy felt for the moment that she wanted to take this big boy on her knee and talk to him for his good. He was only an overgrown lad. But so exceedingly overgrown! Tommy had to content herself with holding out her hand. Dick Danvers grasped it tightly.

Clodd was the only one who did not approve of him.

"How did you get hold of him?" asked Clodd one afternoon, he and Peter alone in the office.

"He came. He came in the usual way," explained Peter.

"What do you know about him?"

"Nothing. What is there to know? One doesn't ask for a character with a journalist."

"No, I suppose that wouldn't work. Found out anything about him since?"

"Nothing against him. Why so suspicious of everybody?"

"Because you are just a woolly lamb and want a dog to look after you. Who is he? On a first night he gives away his stall and sneaks into the pit. When you send him to a picture-gallery, he dodges the private view and goes on the first shilling day. If an invitation comes to a public dinner, he asks me to go and eat it for him and tell him what it's all about. That doesn't suggest the frank and honest journalist, does it?"

"It is unusual, it certainly is unusual," Peter was bound to admit.

"I distrust the man," said Clodd. "He's not our class. What is he doing here?"

"I will ask him, Clodd; I will ask him straight out."

"And believe whatever he tells you."

"No, I shan't."

"Then what's the good of asking him?"

"Well, what am I to do?" demanded the bewildered Peter.

"Get rid of him," suggested Clodd.

"Get rid of him?"

"Get him away! Don't have him in and out of the office all day long-looking at her with those collie-dog eyes of his, arguing art and poetry with her in that cushat-dove voice of his. Get him clean away—if it isn't too late already."

"Nonsense," said Peter, who had turned white, however. "She's not that sort of girl."

"Not that sort of girl!" Clodd had no patience with Peter Hope, and told him so. "Why are there never inkstains on her fingers now? There used to be. Why does she always keep a lemon in her drawer? When did she last have her hair cut? I'll tell you if you care to know—the week before he came, five months ago. She used to have it cut once a fortnight: said it tickled her neck. Why does she jump on people when they call her Tommy and tell them that her name is Jane? It never used to be Jane. Maybe when you're a bit older you'll begin to notice things for yourself."

Clodd jammed his hat on his head and flung himself down the stairs.

Peter, slipping out a minute later, bought himself an ounce of snuff.

"Fiddle-de-dee!" said Peter as he helped himself to his thirteenth pinch. "Don't believe it. I'll sound her. I shan't say a word—I'll just sound her."

Peter stood with his back to the fire. Tommy sat at her desk, correcting proofs of a fanciful story: *The Man Without a Past.*

"I shall miss him," said Peter; "I know I shall."

"Miss whom?" demanded Tommy.

"Danvers," sighed Peter. "It always happens so. You get friendly with a man; then he goes away—abroad, back to America, Lord knows where. You never see him again."

Tommy looked up. There was trouble in her face.

"How do you spell 'harassed'?" questioned Tommy! "two r's or one."

"One r," Peter informed her, "two s's."

"I thought so." The trouble passed from Tommy's face.

"You don't ask when he's going, you don't ask where he's going," complained Peter. "You don't seem to be interested in the least."

"I was going to ask, so soon as I had finished correcting this sheet," explained Tommy. "What reason does he give?"

Peter had crossed over and was standing where he could see her face illumined by the lamplight.

"It doesn't upset you—the thought of his going away, of your never seeing him again?"

"Why should it?" Tommy answered his searching gaze with a slightly puzzled look. "Of course, I'm sorry. He was becoming useful. But we couldn't expect him to stop with us always, could we?"

Peter, rubbing his hands, broke into a chuckle. "I told him 'twas all fiddlesticks. Clodd, he would have it you were growing to care for the fellow."

"For Dick Danvers?" Tommy laughed. "Whatever put that into his head?"

"Oh, well, there were one or two little things that we had noticed."

"We?"

"I mean that Clodd had noticed."

I'm glad it was Clodd that noticed them, not you, dad, thought Tommy to herself. They'd have been pretty obvious if you had noticed them.

"It naturally made me anxious," confessed Peter. "You see, we know absolutely nothing of the fellow."

"Absolutely nothing," agreed Tommy.

"He may be a man of the highest integrity. Personally, I think he is. I like him. On the other hand, he may be a thorough-paced scoundrel. I don't believe for a moment that he is, but he may be. Impossible to say."

"Quite impossible," agreed Tommy.

"Considered merely as a journalist, it doesn't matter. He writes well. He has brains. There's an end of it."

"He is very painstaking," agreed Tommy.

"Personally," added Peter, "I like the fellow." Tommy had returned to her work.

Of what use was Peter in a crisis of this kind? Peter couldn't scold. Peter couldn't bully. The only person to talk to Tommy as Tommy knew she needed to be talked to was one Jane, a young woman of dignity with sense of the proprieties.

"I do hope that at least you are feeling ashamed of yourself," remarked Jane to Tommy that same night, as the twain sat together in their little bedroom.

"Done nothing to be ashamed of," growled Tommy.

"Making a fool of yourself openly, for everybody to notice."

"Clodd ain't everybody. He's got eyes at the back of his head. Sees things before they happen."

"Where's your woman's pride: falling in love with a man who has never spoken to you, except in terms of the most ordinary courtesy."

"I'm not in love with him."

"A man about whom you know absolutely nothing."

"Not in love with him."

"Where does he come from? Who is he?"

"I don't know, don't care; nothing to do with me."

"Just because of his soft eyes, and his wheedling voice, and that half-caressing, half-devotional manner of his. Do you imagine he keeps it specially for you? I gave you credit for more sense."

"I'm not in love with him, I tell you. He's down on his luck, and I'm sorry for him, that's all."

"And if he is, whose fault was it, do you think?"

"It doesn't matter. We are none of us saints. He's trying to pull himself together, and I respect him for it. It's our duty to be charitable and kind to one another in this world!"

"Oh, well, I'll tell you how you can be kind to him: by pointing out to him that he is wasting his time. With his talents, now that he knows his business, he could be on the staff of some big paper, earning a good income. Put it nicely to him, but be firm. Insist on his going. That will be showing true kindness to him—and to yourself, too, I'm thinking, my dear."

And Tommy understood and appreciated the sound good sense underlying Jane's advice, and the very next day but one, seizing the first opportunity, acted upon it; and all would have gone as contemplated if only Dick Danvers had sat still and listened, as it had been arranged in Tommy's programme that he should.

"But I don't want to go," said Dick.

"But you ought to want to go. Staying here with us you are doing yourself no good."

He rose and came to where she stood with one foot upon the fender, looking down into the fire. His doing this disconcerted her.

So long as he remained seated at the other end of the room, she was the sub-editor, counselling the staff for its own good. Now that she could not raise her eyes without encountering his, she felt painfully conscious of being nothing more important than a little woman who was trembling.

"It is doing me all the good in the world," he told her, "being near to you."

"Oh, please do sit down again," she urged him. "I can talk to you so much better when you're sitting down."

But he would not do anything he should have done that day. Instead he took her hands in his, and would not let them go; and the reason and the will went out of her, leaving her helpless.

"Let me be with you always," he pleaded. "It means the difference between light and darkness to me. You have done so much for me. Will you not finish your work? Will you not trust me? It is no hot passion that can pass away, my love for you. It springs from all that is best in me—from the part of me that is wholesome and joyous and strong, the part of me that belongs to you."

Releasing her, he turned away.

"The other part of me—the blackguard—it is dead, dear,—dead and buried. I did not know I was a blackguard, I thought myself a fine fellow, till one day it came home to me. Suddenly I saw myself as I really was. And the sight of the thing frightened me and I ran away from it. I said to myself I would begin life afresh, in a new country, free of every tie that could bind me to the past. It would mean poverty—privation, maybe, in the beginning. What of that? The struggle would brace me. It would be good sport. Ah, well, you can guess the result: the awakening to the cold facts, the reaction of feeling. In what way was I worse than other men? Who was I, to play the prig in a world where others were laughing and dining? I had tramped your city till my boots were worn into holes. I had but to abandon my quixotic ideals—return to where shame lay waiting for me, to be welcomed with the fatted calf. It would have ended so had I not chanced to pass by your door that afternoon and hear you strumming on the piano."

So Billy was right, after all, thought Tommy to herself, the piano does help.

"It was so incongruous—a piano in Crane Court—I looked to see where the noise came from. I read the name of the paper on the doorpost. 'It will be my last chance,' I said to myself. 'This shall decide it.'"

He came back to her. She had not moved. "I am not afraid to tell you all this. You are so big-hearted, so human; you will understand, you can forgive. It is all past. Loving you tells a man that he has done with evil. Will you not trust me?"

She put her hands in his. "I am trusting you," she said, "with all my life. Don't make a muddle of it, dear, if you can help it."

It was an odd wooing, as Tommy laughingly told herself when she came to think it over in her room that night. But that is how it shaped itself.

What troubled her most was that he had not been quite frank with Peter, so that Peter had to defend her against herself.

"I attacked you so suddenly," explained Peter, "you had not time to think. You acted from instinct. A woman seeks to hide her love even from herself."

"I expect, after all, I am more of a girl than a boy," feared Tommy: "I seem to have so many womanish failings."

Peter took himself into quite places and trained himself to face the fact that another would be more to her than he had ever been, and Clodd went about his work like a bear with a sore head; but they neither of them need have troubled themselves so much. The marriage did not take place till nearly fifteen years had passed away, and much water had to flow beneath old London Bridge before that day.

The past is not easily got rid of. A tale was once written of a woman who killed her babe and buried it in a lonely wood, and later stole back in the night and saw there, white in the moonlight, a child's hand calling through the earth, and buried it again and yet again; but always that white baby hand called upwards through the earth, trample it down as she would. Tommy read the story one evening in an old miscellany, and sat long before the dead fire, the book open on her lap, and shivered; for now she knew the fear that had been haunting her.

Tommy lived expecting her. She came one night when Tommy was alone, working late in the office. Tommy knew her the moment she entered the door, a handsome woman, with snake-like, rustling skirts. She closed the door behind her, and drawing forward a chair, seated herself the other side of the desk, and the two looked long and anxiously at one another.

"They told me I should find you here alone," said the woman. "It is better, is it not?"

"Yes," said Tommy, "it is better."

"Tell me," said the woman, "are you very much in love with him?"

"Why should I tell you?"

"Because, if not—if you have merely accepted him thinking him a good catch—which he isn't, my dear; hasn't a penny to bless himself with, and never will if he marries you—why, then the matter is soon settled. They tell me you are a business-like young lady, and I am prepared to make a business-like proposition."

There was no answer. The woman shrugged her shoulders.

"If, on the other hand, you are that absurd creature, a young girl in love—why, then, I suppose we shall have to fight for him."

"It would be more sporting, would it not?" suggested Tommy.

"Let me explain before you decide," continued the woman. "Dick Danvers left me six months ago, and has kept from me ever since, because he loved me."

"It sounds a curious reason."

"I was a married woman when Dick Danvers and I first met. Since he left me—for my sake and his own—I have received information of my husband's death."

"And does Dick—does he know?" asked the girl.

"Not yet. I have only lately learnt the news myself."

"Then if it is as you say, when he knows he will go back to you."

"There are difficulties in the way."

"What difficulties?"

"My dear, this. To try and forget me, he has been making love to you. Men do these things. I merely ask you to convince yourself of the truth. Go away for six months—disappear entirely. Leave him free—uninfluenced. If he loves you—if it be not merely a sense of honour that binds him—you will find him here on your return. If not—if in the interval I have succeeded in running off with him, well, is not the two or three thousand pounds I am prepared to put into this paper of yours a fair price for such a lover?"

Tommy rose with a laugh of genuine amusement. She could never altogether put aside her sense of humour, let Fate come with what terrifying face it would.

"You may have him for nothing—if he is that man," the girl told her; "he shall be free to choose between us."

"You mean you will release him from his engagement?"

"That is what I mean."

"Why not take my offer? You know the money is needed. It will save your father years of anxiety and struggle. Go away—travel, for a couple of months, if you're afraid of the six. Write him that you must be alone, to think things over."

The girl turned upon her.

"And leave you a free field to lie and trick?"

The woman, too, had risen. "Do you think he really cares for you? At the moment you interest him. At nineteen every woman is a mystery. When the mood is past—and do you know how long a man's mood lasts, you poor chit? Till he has caught what he is running after, and has tasted it—then he will think not of what he has won, but of what he has lost: of the society from which he has cut himself adrift; of all the old pleasures and pursuits he can no longer enjoy; of the luxuries—necessities to a man of his stamp—that marriage with you has deprived him of. Then your face will be a perpetual reminder to him of what he has paid for it, and he will curse it every time he sees it."

"You don't know him," the girl cried. "You know just a part of him—the part you would know. All the rest of him is a good man, that would rather his self-respect than all the luxuries you mention—you included."

"It seems to resolve itself into what manner of man he is," laughed the woman.

The girl looked at her watch. "He will be here shortly; he shall tell us himself."

"How do you mean?"

"That here, between the two of us, he shall decide—this very night." She showed her white face to the woman. "Do you think I could live through a second day like to this?"

"The scene would be ridiculous."

"There will be none here to enjoy the humour of it."

"He will not understand."

"Oh, yes, he will," the girl laughed. "Come, you have all the advantages; you are rich, you are clever; you belong to his class. If he elects to stop with me, it will be because he is my man—mine. Are you afraid?"

The woman shivered. She wrapped her fur cloak about her closer and sat down again, and Tommy returned to her proofs. It was press-night, and there was much to be done.

He came a little later, though how long the time may have seemed to the two women one cannot say. They heard his footstep on the stair. The woman rose and went forward, so that when he opened the door she was the first he saw. But he made no sign. Possibly he had been schooling himself for this moment, knowing that sooner or later it must come. The woman held out her hand to him with a smile.

"I have not the honour," he said.

The smile died from her face. "I do not understand," she said.

"I have not the honour," he repeated. "I do not know you."

The girl was leaning with her back against the desk in a somewhat mannish attitude. He stood between them. It will always remain Life's chief comic success: the man between two women. The situation has amused the world for so many years. Yet, somehow, he contrived to maintain a certain dignity.

"Maybe," he continued, "you are confounding me with a Dick Danvers who lived in New York up to a few months ago. I knew him well—a worthless scamp you had done better never to have met."

"You bear a wonderful resemblance to him," laughed the woman.

"The poor fool is dead," he answered. "And he left for you, my dear lady, this dying message: that, from the bottom of his soul, he was sorry for the wrong he had done you. He asked you to forgive him—and forget him."

"The year appears to be opening unfortunately for me," said the woman. "First my lover, then my husband."

He had nerved himself to fight the living. This was a blow from the dead. The man had been his friend.

"Dead?"

"He was killed, it appears, in that last expedition in July," answered the woman. "I received the news from the Foreign Office only a fortnight ago."

An ugly look came into his eyes—the look of a cornered creature fighting for its life. "Why have you followed me here? Why do I find you here alone with her? What have you told her?"

The woman shrugged her shoulders. "Only the truth."

"All the truth?" he demanded—"all? Ah! be just. Tell her it was not all my fault. Tell her all the truth."

"What would you have me tell her? That I played Potiphar's wife to your Joseph?"

"Ah, no! The truth—only the truth. That you and I were a pair of idle fools with the devil dancing round us. That we played a fool's game, and that it is over."

"Is it over? Dick, is it over?" She flung her arms towards him; but he threw her from him almost brutally. "The man is dead, I tell you. His folly and his sin lie dead with him. I have nothing to do with you, nor you with me."

"Dick!" she whispered. "Dick, cannot you understand? I must speak with you alone."

But they did not understand, neither the man nor the child.

"Dick, are you really dead?" she cried. "Have you no pity for me? Do you think that I have followed you here to grovel at your feet for mere whim? Am I acting like a woman sane and sound? Don't you see that I am mad, and why I am mad? Must I tell you before her? Dick—" She staggered towards him, and the fine cloak slipped from her shoulders; and then it was that Tommy changed from a child into a woman, and raised the other woman from the ground with crooning words of encouragement such as mothers use, and led her to the inner room. "Do not go," she said, turning to Dick; "I shall be back in a few minutes."

He crossed to one of the windows against which beat the City's roar, and it seemed to him as the throb of passing footsteps beating down through the darkness to where he lay in his grave.

She re-entered, closing the door softly behind her. "It is true?" she asked.

"It can be. I had not thought of it."

They spoke in low, matter-of-fact tones, as people do who have grown weary of their own emotions.

"When did he go away—her husband?"

"About—it is February now, is it not? About eighteen months ago."

"And died just eight months ago. Rather conveniently, poor fellow."

"Yes, I'm glad he is dead—poor Lawrence."

"What is the shortest time in which a marriage can be arranged?"

"I do not know," he answered listlessly. "I do not intend to marry her."

"You would leave her to bear it alone?"

"It is not as if she were a poor woman. You can do anything with money."

"It will not mend reputation. Her position in society is everything to that class of woman."

"My marrying her now," he pointed out, "would not save her."

"Practically speaking it would," the girl pleaded. "The world does not go out of its way to find out things it does not want to know. Marry her as quietly as possible and travel for a year or two."

"Why should I? Ah! it is easy enough to call a man a coward for defending himself against a woman. What is he to do when he is fighting for his life? Men do not sin with good women."

"There is the child to be considered," she urged—"your child. You see, dear, we all do wrong sometimes. We must not let others suffer for our fault more—more than we can help."

He turned to her for the first time. "And you?"

"I? Oh, I shall cry for a little while, but later on I shall laugh, as often. Life is not all love. I have my work."

He knew her well by this time. And also it came to him that it would be a finer thing to be worthy of her than even to possess her.

So he did her bidding and went out with the other woman. Tommy was glad it was press-night. She would not be able to think for hours to come, and then, perhaps, she would be feeling too tired. Work can be very kind.

Were this an artistic story, here, of course, one would write "Finis." But in the workaday world one never knows the ending till it comes. Had it been otherwise, I doubt I could have found courage to tell you this story of Tommy. It is not all true—at least, I do not suppose so. One drifts unconsciously a little way into dream-land when one sits oneself down to recall the happenings of long ago; while Fancy, with a sly wink, whispers ever and again to Memory: "Let me tell this incident—picture that scene: I can make it so much more interesting than you would." But Tommy—how can I put it without saying too much: there is someone I think of when I speak of her? To remember only her dear wounds, and not the healing of them, would have been a task too painful. I love to dwell on their next meeting. Flipp, passing him on the steps, did not know him, the tall, sunburnt gentleman with the sweet, grave-faced little girl.

"Seen that face somewhere before," mused Flipp, as at the corner of Bedford Street he climbed into a hansom, "seen it somewhere on a thinner man."

For Dick Danvers, that he did not recognise Flipp, there was more excuse. A very old young man had Flipp become at thirty. Flipp no longer enjoyed popular journalism. He produced it.

The gold-bound doorkeeper feared the mighty Clodd would be unable to see so insignificant an atom as an unappointed stranger, but would let the card of Mr. Richard Danvers plead for itself. To the gold-bound keeper's surprise came down the message that Mr. Danvers was to be at once shown up.

"I thought, somehow, you would come to me first," said the portly Clodd, advancing with out-stretched hand. "And this is—?"

"My little girl, Honor. We have been travelling for the last few months."

Clodd took the grave, small face between his big, rough hands:

"Yes. She is like you. But looks as if she were going to have more sense. Forgive me, I knew your father my dear," laughed Clodd; "when he was younger."

They lit their cigars and talked.

"Well, not exactly dead; we amalgamated it," winked Clodd in answer to Danvers' inquiry. "It was just a trifle *too* high-class. Besides, the old gentleman was not getting younger. It hurt him a little at first. But then came Tommy's great success, and that has reconciled him to all things. Do they know you are in England?"

"No," explained Danvers; "we arrived only last night."

Clodd called directions down the speaking-tube.

"You will find hardly any change in her. One still has to keep one's eye upon her chin. She has not even lost her old habit of taking stock of people. You remember." Clodd laughed.

They talked a little longer, till there came a whistle, and Clodd put his ear to the tube.

"I have to see her on business," said Clodd, rising; "you may as well come with me. They are still in the old place, Gough Square."

Tommy was out, but Peter was expecting her every minute.

Peter did not know Dick, but would not admit it. Forgetfulness was a sign of age, and Peter still felt young.

"I know your face quite well," said Peter; "can't put a name to it, that's all."

Clodd whispered it to him, together with information bringing history up to date. And then light fell upon the old lined face. He came towards Dick, meaning to take him by both hands, but, perhaps because he had become somewhat feeble, he seemed glad when the younger man put his arms around him and held him for a moment. It was un-English, and both of them felt a little ashamed of themselves afterwards.

"What we want," said Clodd, addressing Peter, "we three—you, I, and Miss Danvers—is tea and cakes, with cream in them; and I know a shop where they sell them. We will call back for your father in half an hour." Clodd explained to Miss Danvers; "he has to talk over a matter of business with Miss Hope."

"I know," answered the grave-faced little person. She drew Dick's face down to hers and kissed it. And then the three went out together, leaving Dick standing by the window.

"Couldn't we hide somewhere till she comes?" suggested Miss Danvers. "I want to see her."

So they waited in the open doorway of a near printing-house till Tommy drove up. Both Peter and Clodd watched the child's face with some anxiety. She nodded gravely to herself three times, then slipped her hand into Peter's.

Tommy opened the door with her latchkey and passed in.